PRAISE FOR *INDIGENE*

"Enitan was introduced two decades ago and her presence remains as compelling today as it was then. Through her journey, readers are invited to see Nigeria in all its beauty and contradictions. Atta's powerful narrative captures the nation's complexities in a way that feels familiar and insightful. It doesn't merely entertain; it also challenges, with an eloquence that is poignant and profound. Beyond that, Atta's stories often serve as a subtle guide to the art of being Nigerian, offering an intricate portrayal of cultural nuances and everyday strategies."

—**Peju Alatise, visual artist and writer**

"A work of brilliance and power. Enitan comes alive yet again, painted with Atta's compassionate brushstrokes, and carries us through a real and very human journey. Atta's prose is nuanced, quietly dazzling, and completely enthralling."

—**Abubakar Adam Ibrahim, journalist and author of** *Season of Crimson Blossoms*

"This beautifully imagined collection turns an astute gaze on Nigeria and its diasporas through arresting snapshots of lives at crossroads. It is unflinching, yet laced with humor, wit and a tenderness that illuminates people and places as only great literature can."

—**Ayọ̀bámi Adébáyọ̀, author of** *Stay With Me* **and** *A Spell of Good Things*

ALSO BY SEFI ATTA

Novels
Everything Good Will Come
Swallow
A Bit of Difference
The Bead Collector
The Bad Immigrant
Good-for-Nothing Girl

Short Stories
News from Home

Plays
Sefi Atta: Selected Plays

INDIGENE

A NOVELLA & SHORT STORIES

By Sefi Atta

Interlink Books

An imprint of Interlink Publishing Group, Inc.
Northampton, Massachusetts

First published in 2025 by

Interlink Books
An imprint of Interlink Publishing Group, Inc.
46 Crosby Street, Northampton, MA 01060
www.interlinkbooks.com

Copyright © Sefi Atta, 2025

An excerpt from *Indigene* was published in *Southeast Review*.
"Unsuitable Ties" first appeared in *Expound*, "Debt" in *NarrativeNortheast* and
"Housekeeping" in *World Literature Today*.

All rights reserved; no part of this publication may be reproduced, stored in a retrieval system, or transmitted, in any form or by any means, electronic, mechanical, photo-copying, recording or otherwise, without the prior written permission of the publisher.

Library of Congress Cataloging-in-Publication data available.
ISBN-13: 978-1-62371-606-6

Printed and bound in China

To Gboyega and Temi Ransome-Kuti,
for divergent and convergent views

"I have been here before. I have passed through this present point again and again. My head is filled with the smells and senses of that other time and with recognition comes the added pain of a repeated leave-taking."
—Wole Soyinka, *The Man Died*

"In place of citizenship, the Nigerian
is reduced to an indigene."
—Dele Farotimi, lawyer,
author and political activist

CONTENTS

Indigene — 11
Unsuitable Ties — 127
Debt — 155
Housekeeping — 177
Acknowledgements — 189

INDIGENE

Her return is long overdue. She must apologize for that and also for being too optimistic the last time she was here. However, Kirikiri Women's Prison is not where she wants to be, this Saturday afternoon in January 2020, to express her regret in person. Her drive from Lekki peninsula to Lagos mainland took almost three hours. She then got stuck in a gridlock caused by the tankers from Apapa Port Complex and is still a little nauseous from inhaling their exhaust fumes. Now that she's finally arrived, skin clammy under her adirẹ tunic and trousers, shoulders strained by the bags of provisions she carries, she is yet again frustrated by the thought that her so-called advocacy for inmates is no more than charity.

The prison looks exactly the same. It formally became a correctional center in August 2019 when President Buhari signed the Nigerian Correctional Service Bill. A sign at the entrance bears its former name above green double doors, one of which has a piece of paper taped to it stating "Visit is free." Enitan herself has never had to bribe anyone to see an inmate, but she is well aware that this is sometimes the case. The woman in charge here is a Christian and has a strict maternal approach to running the place. She makes sure rules are followed and inmates are treated fairly. They call her Mama, and she refers to them as her children or residents.

Two officials in green berets and khaki shirts and trousers welcome Enitan in unison as she walks through the doors.

"Happy New Year, ma!"

"Same to you," Enitan says.

Her gray hair is in a shuku bun. She wears glasses that magnify her laughter lines as she returns their smiles. One is an officer and the other a warder. Armed male guards stand nearby, and on the wall ahead is a quote by Maya Angelou: "I can be changed by what happens to me, but I refuse to be reduced by it." And another by Benjamin Franklin: "Be always at war with your vices, at peace with your neighbors and let each new year find you a better man."

The warder adjusts her belt under her potbelly. "Long time."

"Yes," Enitan says. "How was your Christmas?"

"Fine, ma. We thank God."

The officer pulls back her beret to scratch her head. "Who are you seeing first today?"

"Blessing."

"That girl. She's been disturbing us over you."

"Really?"

"Don't mind her. Maybe she thinks you're her mate."

The officer gives Enitan a pat down and checks her bags of provisions, which contain toiletries and sanitary towels. She would ask Enitan to hand over her phone at this point, if Enitan didn't always leave it in her car.

The warder beckons. "Follow me."

Enitan finds relief in the warder's nonchalant stroll. She is familiar with the cracks and pockmarks in the cement floor of the corridor, the peels and scratches on the emulsion-painted walls, the slight odor of Dettol by the staff toilet door and the distant voices of inmates.

Kirikiri is a group of penal facilities named after the town they are located in. The buildings are colonial bungalows with exteriors that have shown Public Works Department durability and interiors that are in dire need of renovation. There's a medium and a maximum security section for men and the one section for women. Statistics change and are hard to substantiate, but the total population is about four thousand. The men's maximum prison is overcrowded by double its capacity, their medium prison is two-thirds occupied, and the women's prison is relatively underutilized, with a fluctuating count of two to three hundred.

The new law gives the state comptroller of prisons a right to reject inmates in congested prisons, and Enitan asks the warder if this is being exercised at the men's maximum prison.

"Me, I don't know," the warder replies, "but they released some last year."

Enitan shakes her head. "They were doing that anyway."

Under the new law, the prisons are expected to reform, rehabilitate, and reintegrate prisoners, as they should. They are also meant to provide them with medical and other services, as they ought to. But Enitan has read newspaper reports about problems that persist in the men's sections. The cells in the maximum prison apparently resemble a concentration camp, and inmates complain their meals are disgusting and their facilities are filthy. They are harassed and assaulted daily by fellow prisoners. If they get injured or fall sick, they have to provide their own medication and supplies, and when they receive gifts or donations from people and organizations on the outside, their officials allegedly pilfer them. Conditions at the men's medium prison are less grim, but there have been past protests over the disparity of treatment between inmates. VIPs, such as the odd corrupt politician and drug lord, are rumored to rent special cells, in which they have their own stoves, fans and electricity generators, and to receive occasional conjugal visits.

In the women's prison, most of the inmates are detainees who were arrested for crimes ranging from theft to murder. Some were falsely accused and others just didn't have any money to bribe the police to release them. Now they've been charged, they can't afford to hire lawyers to apply for bail as they await their trials. The majority of them are sex workers in their twenties, and among the others, three were pregnant on admission and five have their children staying with them. Inmates wear casual clothes and are housed in dormitories and sleep on bunk beds. They have a crèche, a library, a health clinic and hair salon. During the day, they attend classes, workshops and prayer services, and within certain hours they're allowed to have visitors—family, friends, religious and advocacy groups, and lawyers like Enitan. Once in a while, celebrities make an appearance and afterward post online photos of themselves at the entrance.

"How come you haven't changed your name?" Enitan asks.

The warder shrugs. "Even if we call it Kirikiri Hotel, it's still a prison."

Indigene

Enitan nods in agreement. Besides the troubling matter of the inmates' prolonged detentions, she hasn't found any evidence that they're mistreated. She hasn't read or heard reports to that effect either, but has no way of knowing how the prison operates in her absence. Her exchanges with officials are at best restrained.

At the back gate, the warder excuses herself and returns to the entrance. Enitan steps out alone into the courtyard, which is bordered on one side by yellow-and-green bungalows and has a designated reconciliation spot for inmates called the Love Garden. Her heartbeat quickens as the soles of her sandals crunch the graveled ground.

It has been twenty-five years since she was arrested for allegedly disobeying public orders during General Abacha's regime. She was at a literary reading that evening, attended by supposed dissidents. State Security agents swarmed the venue, claiming the writers and audience were participating in unlawful political activities. She and her host, Grace Ameh, a journalist, were subsequently detained. She was thirty-five and pregnant with her daughter, Yimika, at the time. The terror that seized her during her overnight stay in the holding cell, and the stench of shit buckets that followed her long after her release, were enough to motivate her to start her prison project, Indigene.

At first, she thought Indigene should focus on expectant mothers and mothers who were locked up with their children, but she found they got more attention, and sympathy, from legal and other organizations dedicated to their cause, so she decided instead to support women who were on death row or serving life terms. One of them came up with the name, which Enitan initially had reservations about, but the inmate said she used it to separate incarcerated prisoners like herself from detainees, whom she called Settlers. Enitan visits the prison three times a year, in December, April and August. Indigene is a part-time endeavor and she doesn't solicit donations for it. She doesn't represent the women either, as her firm specializes in commercial law. Apart from providing them with provisions, she sits with them and listens to their grievances. They tend to be overlooked by outsiders because they are convicted murderers and have no chance of getting out. There are eight of them in all, and Blessing, who has recently turned twenty-two, is the youngest.

Blessing is in a sulky mood when they meet in the reception area where inmates receive visitors. She is like this at times and can be demanding. The area, as usual, has been dusted down and swept clean. It has wooden benches and windows that allow a through draft and provide views of the palm trees and almond trees surrounding the premises. Other inmates and visitors are present and the warder on duty stands by as they carry on conversations in tones that would befit a funeral parlor.

"You didn't even come and see me at Christmas," Blessing says.

She has a disarmingly timid voice and sometimes seems conscious of her diction. Pretty, with upturned eyes, she is unrecognizable from the media photos in which her face is plastered with makeup and her forehead is covered with a wig. Today she sports didi braids and wears cut-out jeans and a knock-off Givenchy T-shirt.

"I'm sorry," Enitan says, her expression contrite. "I was busy."

She has taken to treating Blessing as a teacher would a student. She has to set boundaries; otherwise, she may leave herself open to manipulation.

Blessing pouts. "Only my mother and brother came."

"What about your father?"

"He disowned me."

"Ah-ah, why?"

"He says I have no conscience."

"Hm. That's a pity."

During Blessing's trial, her lawyer alleged that she'd stabbed her victim with a steak knife as he attempted to rape her. She was a second-year student at University of Lagos, and he was a senior bank executive and married with children. They were in a hotel room when the incident occurred. The prosecution established that he and Blessing were having an affair. They had corroborative text messages, which were exposed in the media, along with Blessing's racy Instagram photos. He had just one photo in circulation, in which he wore a business suit and was surrounded by his employees. He was referred to as a family man while Blessing was called a runs girl. Her father initially professed her innocence, going as far as to say she went to the hotel to experience what it was like to have a room-service meal.

"I met Auntie Isioma," Blessing says.

Enitan frowns. "Auntie Isioma?"

"The lawyer who bails people."

"Oh, her!"

"She says she knows you."

"Yes, yes, we do know each other. She came here?"

"In December. She wants to mentor me."

Enitan hesitates. "That's good. I didn't know she was mentoring as well."

Blessing explains that Isioma started a mentoring program for female prisoners, which will begin this year. She won't mentor them herself but will connect them to a group of professional women she belongs to.

Enitan nods encouragingly. Blessing and Isioma are Igbo. She doesn't know if they're from the same state or locality, but Blessing would have more in common with Isioma than with Enitan—their language, for one. Enitan and Isioma have never met in the course of carrying out their prison projects, but perhaps Isioma has come to realize that bailing out detainees is a never-ending task.

"Do you know your mentor?" Enitan asks.

"Not yet," Blessing says.

"It would be interesting to find out who she is," Enitan says.

She is fairly well acquainted with the group Isioma referred to. The women are qualified professionals all right, but some of the founders married wealthy men and never had noteworthy careers. Better known for flying first class around the globe to shop or visit their children in boarding schools and universities abroad, they are now at that hazardous middle-aged phase in their lives. They're either bored with their Chanel and whatnot, or their lifestyles can't sustain their longings to be admired and revered, so they turn their attention to social causes—child abuse, girls' education, women's empowerment, this and that. She calls them ladies who launch.

Isioma is in a different category. Ten or so years younger, she grew up in Enugu and settled in Lagos after law school. She is blatantly aspirational, as out-of-towners can be, and associates herself with society people she ought to disregard, such as the ladies who launch. She married a man from an old Lagos family. They had two sons and later divorced when his father's estate got caught up in a will contest that carried on for years, during which he was too entitled to get a job. She has since had to be resourceful to maintain her financial status.

Blessing continues. "She wants to raise awareness about what is happening to me."

"Yes?"

"She thinks I've been treated unfairly."

Enitan guesses that Blessing is repeating Isioma verbatim here. Isioma "raises awareness" and "fights causes." She is in "the activism space." This type of American talk is all too common in Nigeria now. So is Isioma's brand of activism, which probably originated in Hollywood.

Isioma approached Enitan at a party a few years ago and said she admired the work Enitan was doing at Indigene. Enitan joked that it wasn't work; it was atonement for being able to get out of detention quickly. Isioma pressed her for details about her experience there, staring at her in wonderment, and ended their conversation by saying she'd like to pick Enitan's brain someday, which sounded like a brutal threat. She did call a couple of times afterward, to ask questions about starting a similar project, then they were out of contact for a while until they met again at a Lagos wedding, where the bride's aṣọ ẹbi colors were a challenging peacock green and citrine yellow that Enitan ignored and Isioma managed to observe. Isioma, without due humility, said she'd set up her own prison project and it was called I, after her initial. Enitan said, "Oh," wondering why anyone would choose such a self-centered name.

Enitan would readily admit she doesn't raise awareness. If people don't care to know what women in prisons go through, that is okay with her. She certainly doesn't fight causes, as there's no use. The more belligerent women activists get in Nigeria, the more the government mocks them or overlooks them for their more softly spoken counterparts. She has never once called herself an activist or described activism in Nigeria as a space.

"I was wrong about your sentence," she says to Blessing. "I honestly didn't expect it."

Blessing looks her in the eye. "Will they hang me?"

Enitan's heartbeat quickens again. "No, they won't."

"But the judge said it in court."

Enitan shakes her head. "Appeal and keep appealing."

She has been through this with Blessing before on the phone. Blessing may not have got a life sentence, as she predicted during her previous visit in August, but death penalties in Nigeria these days are nearly always delayed indefinitely, and the new laws give the chief judge the right to commute them to life terms after a period of ten years has elapsed. This is all Blessing can hope for now.

Before her arrest, Blessing was studying mass communication and working part-time at a radio station. She ran errands for the CEO. How she got the job with him was one matter. What errands she was running for him was another, but through him she met the victim, who worked in the marketing and communications department of a bank. Blessing wanted to be an On-Air Personality, with a view to branding herself like *Big Brother Naija* contestants.

When Blessing's sentence was announced in November last year, Enitan called her and afterward spoke to her lawyer, Tunji Banjoko, from the Office of the Public Defender. Tunji was accustomed to and competent at handling murder trials but wasn't prepared for one as high profile as Blessing's—one that was said to be all over the Internet and labeled a case of trial by media. His office didn't have the wherewithal to counteract the public's impression of Blessing, while he didn't have the sensitivity to deal with her. He found her cold, and thought that may have put off the judge, a woman who had previously shown more leniency in sentencing convicted murderers. Enitan said "numb" was a better assessment of Blessing's state of mind, but on second thought, she was unsure. Did the media attention detach Blessing from the trial, or was the experience for her rather like being the star of a reality show?

"Auntie Isioma even promised to help me clean up my image," Blessing says.

"That's fine," Enitan says, keeping a straight face. "But try not to do or say anything that will make you look bad."

Why the sudden interest in Blessing? she wonders. Why the poking around and offering PR services? Isioma is not wishy-washy that way. She is intentional—not just about her associations but about her appearance, and her accent, which may give unsuspecting listeners the impression she was educated in England. She is particularly shrewd when it comes to her career.

Enitan isn't surprised that Isioma came all the way here. Isioma would want to appear serious about her mentoring project, unlike the ladies who launch. They would rather promote themselves in the media and collect dubious national honors, in the hope of receiving invitations to speak at the UN and similar organizations, but they are very clear about where their preoccupation with human rights ends. They won't cross the bridge from Lagos Island to visit any prisoner. Enitan is sure they're happy to be identified as mentors, regardless. They patronize women like Isioma who have time for them and begrudge anyone who willfully refuses to look up to them.

Enitan could easily be part of their social circle, so they can't accuse her of envy, which is their go-to defense, but she does sometimes wonder if she's that different from them.

Blessing, she suspects, is merely trying to get back at her for skipping her Christmas visit by mentioning Isioma, yet she finds it hard to pay her no mind. She cares about Indigenes—not to the extent that she would about a close relative or friend, but in the same way. She excuses their flaws and hopes they do hers. Sometimes she withholds opinions, so as not to upset them. She won't lie to them, though, and makes sure she researches their cases and meets them several times beforehand to see if they can develop a rapport. Inmates are liable to mistrust her because of her background. She can't bring herself to deal with convicts who have murdered children, and she must believe they murdered in self-defense. She still doesn't know what to make of the fact that they've all killed men. None of them is given to misandry, and she would be put off by that. As for their fatal acts of violence, she is just grateful she's never been in a position that would cause her to take another person's life.

Blessing has been having a difficult time with other inmates since her sentencing. She rows with them and resents having to settle disagreements in the Love Garden. She is especially annoyed by an older inmate who she says has it in for her.

"Did she tell you that?" Enitan asks, worried that Blessing may be at risk of physical harm.

Blessing raises her voice. "No, but she's always trying to provoke me!"

They get the attention of the warder, who has so far seemed indifferent to their conversation. Enitan wonders if Blessing spoke loudly on purpose.

"How?" she asks.

Blessing says the older inmate calls her Slay Queen, not as a compliment, and stares her down whenever they pass each other.

"Just ignore her," Enitan says, even though she would find it aggravating to be in that position.

"I do," Blessing says. "I've left it in God's hands. It's God that will judge her."

Blessing is Catholic and practices her religion faithfully these days. She prays with rosary beads and recites novenas. Enitan would be amused by the irony of her belief in divine justice if the circumstances were appropriate.

Her session is over. Blessing leaves the reception area and Augustina struts in flexing her biceps. Augustina, a thirty-five-year-old Ibibio woman, is a table tennis champ and belongs to a self-appointed group that breaks up dorm fights. She wears a sleeveless muscle T and knee-length shorts and has a new buzz cut.

"Big Sis!" she says.

"Tin Tin," Enitan says. "Na you be dis?"

"Na me, o," Augustina says, rubbing her head. "I shaved de whole Goddam."

Enitan laughs. Augustina had an Afro the last time Enitan saw her. A popular woman, she alleviates the atmosphere in the reception area, drawing fond glances from other inmates and curious stares from their visitors. Unfazed, she sits down with her legs wide apart and grins. "How body?"

"I dey," Enitan says. "How you dey?"

Augustina immediately divulges that she's been through early menopause and describes her symptoms in pidgin—her mind no rest, her body dey sweat for night and she no fit sleep well.

"No bring me sanitary towel again," she says. "I no need am. It be like say every tin done dry finish."

"Eh-yah," Enitan says.

She relies on sounds when she can't find the right words to express sympathy. She welcomed menopause when it began for her. If nothing else, it gave her an excuse to be less accommodating.

Augustina killed her husband, an alcoholic who habitually beat her up because she couldn't have children. The day she told him she was leaving him, he smashed a beer bottle against the wall, with the intention of scarring her face so no other man would want her. She struggled with him and he pushed her to the floor. She grabbed a shard of the beer bottle and jabbed him in the chest before he could cut her. The man bled to death on their way to the nearest hospital. Augustina said it wasn't her fault there were none where they lived.

After her, Enitan sees other Indigenes who are serving life terms and have over the years found ways to carry on. She can't fathom how they're able to, and with spirit that astounds her.

Her final session is with Sikira, who is forty-four but could pass for a sixty-year-old because of her pronounced air of solemnity. A Lagos Muslim, Sikira wears a black boubou and scarf. In her spare time, she braids hair and teaches Koranic lessons. Inmates come to her for advice. They call her Auntie SK. The kind of Yoruba woman to expect a great deal of respect from her juniors, she shows as much of it to her seniors and goes through the whole rigmarole of curtsying and exchanging formal greetings with Enitan.

"Ẹku ọjọ mẹta," she says.

"Ọjọ kan pẹlu," Enitan replies with a smile.

Sikira never has much to say about prison life, but gives updates on her siblings and parents. Her father has been ill and her siblings are having trouble paying for his treatment.

"Sometimes I think I'm lucky to be here," she concludes. "At least I don't have to think about food and rent."

"Don't say that," Enitan mumbles. "Don't say that at all."

She can't always make comforting sounds. She can't afford to give financial assistance whenever an Indigene tells her about their family problems either, so she offers prayers, to which Sikira repeatedly answers, "Amin."

Sikira killed her landlord. She owed him rent and when he knocked on her room door one evening she opened it to find him standing there with an iron pole in his hand. She darted back in and he chased after her. An elderly man, he was known for threatening his tenants, but never once followed through. Sikira claimed she wasn't aware of this. She grabbed the pole from him and banged him on the head with it. He collapsed, and no one in the entire building could resuscitate him.

Always considerate, Sikira attempts to end Enitan's visit earlier than planned.

"You look tired today, ma," she says, lowering her gaze.

"Do I?" Enitan asks, with a smile.

Sikira briefly studies her face sideways. "Yes."

"I'm fine," Enitan says. "Maybe it was the traffic on my way."

"Coming here can't be easy."

"It wasn't always this bad."

"My family, too, complain. I tell them not to bother."

"Why?" Enitan asks. "If they want to see you, let them."

She would like to add that Sikira shouldn't worry so much about her family, but Sikira might take offense and, though polite, won't back down if she believes she's right. Sikira won't even accept she deserves company for a few more minutes and continues to persuade her to leave. Enitan finally gives in, and they both stand up.

"Send your family my greetings," she says.

"I will," Sikira says, with a curtsy.

Enitan thanks the warder and strides out of the reception area as if it's possible to escape what she's heard. She isn't as tired as she appears. She walks regularly for exercise and has more stamina than she had when she started Indigene, but her visits to Kirikiri no longer make sense. The traffic will be worse on her way back, and by the time she gets home, she would have spent more hours on the road than she has here.

Yimika is on her laptop when Enitan gets home at about seven thirty in the evening. She doesn't appear to be at work, sprawled on the gray sectional sofa in the main room and dressed in a rumpled yellow T-shirt and faded denim shorts, but she may well be.

"Hey, Mum," she murmurs.

"Hey, Yim-Yim," Enitan says.

The air conditioner is on, and the flat smells mildly of mosquito repellant. She is used to walking in on her daughter like this and has learned not to speak until she's spoken to, in case she interrupts an online meeting. Sometimes she calls her Yim-Yim and other times Yimz. People often remark that they look alike, but all they have in common are their complexions and smiles.

"How did it go?" Yimika asks, gathering her waist-length braids to one side.

Enitan sighs. "Not very well."

"Uh, why not?"

Enitan is about to reply when she notices an empty bowl with a fork and stew smears—what is left of pounded yam and egusi. Yimika will even eat it for breakfast and has left the bowl propped up on a folded tea cloth at a corner of the center table.

"Yimz," she says, "how many times must I tell you not to do this?"

Yimika glances at the bowl. "Oops, sorry."

"Please take it to the kitchen."

Yimika stretches before reaching for the bowl and tea cloth, which she holds so clumsily as she stands up that the fork somersaults to the floor.

"What the . . ." she mutters.

The fork bounces and lands. For a moment, Yimika looks confused.

"You could try picking it up," Enitan says.

Yimika laughs as she bends forward. "Calm down. I was about to."

She retrieves the fork and heads to the kitchen as Enitan plonks herself on the sectional, kicks off her shoes and searches the room for more evidence of mess, but can't find any.

Home, for them, is an estate on Admiralty Way in Lekki Phase One, raised above street level to avoid perennial floods. They share a generator, water pump and treatment plant with other residents, for which Enitan pays a steep annual service charge. Their flat is on the top floor and overlooks Five Cowries Creek. Apart from the main room, which has a dining and lounging section, it has three bedrooms and a guest room that serves as a home office they rarely use. The floors are tiled throughout, and the walls are decorated with paintings that Enitan bought at Lekki arts and crafts market.

When she first viewed the flat, she foolishly visualized herself sitting on the balcony after work on evenings like this, gazing at the creek and drinking homemade lemongrass tea. She did that one time only. Mosquitoes bit her from head to toe and the traffic on Admiralty Way was far too loud—horns beeping, engines roaring and sirens going off. Then there was the armed robbery at a bank across the road, carried out by a gang who arrived by boat on the creek, in broad daylight. That stopped her from staying longer than five minutes on her balcony, "before someone shoots my head off," she joked to her colleagues the morning after the incident.

She bought the flat primarily because it was near Yimika's crèche and school, both of which had after-hours programs. She did school runs herself, refusing to entrust Yimika to a nanny and driver as other working mothers she knew did. She had house help all right, but she wasn't taking any chances. The location also gave her an alternative route to work, as well as proximity to the two people she saw regularly—her father, Sunny Taiwo, and her long-term partner, Ladi Akinsanya. She took them into consideration as well, so she wouldn't spend most of her time in traffic. To visit her father, she could easily take the link bridge to Ikoyi, which was within walking distance. Ladi's medical clinic was a ten-minute drive from her estate and his house was fifteen minutes away. Both locations were in her part of Lekki and accessible by side roads.

She hasn't quite dropped off the Lagos social scene, but she doesn't attend as many functions as she did when she was married to her ex-husband, Niyi Franco. This is partly due to their divorce. In his most petty phase, Niyi set about trying to "sully," as she wrote in a strongly worded email to him, "her reputation." She couldn't help herself. She retaliated with pettiness of her own, which included cutting off mutual friends who suggested she shouldn't have left him because he hadn't beaten her or cheated on her. She never bothered to explain her position. She had a baby to look after and was emotionally exhausted. It was public knowledge that her father had been detained by Abacha's regime anyway, so if a handful of people truly believed she was eager to get involved in the pro-democracy movement while she was pregnant and at risk of miscarrying, that was their problem. She wasn't exactly charging around Lagos with placards. All she did was talk to a few journalists about her father's disappearance, which was the least she could do. It wasn't Niyi's place to try and stop her, and he needn't have slandered her either. She never had a great reputation as his wife, notorious as she was for her unwillingness to cook.

Yimika returns from the kitchen and resumes her work. She is in Lagos temporarily. She shares a house in London with friends and plans to head back in April. She quit her previous job there and is now employed by a start-up that is about to launch a website and app called Home Pro, through which Nigerians can hire plumbers, electricians and other artisans, as they call themselves. Enitan, who relies on dodgy word-of-mouth recommendations, welcomes the idea.

The estate they live in was advertised as a new build when she first heard of it, but before she moved in, she had to pay for further work on the flat. The walls were badly smudged and she got them repainted. The light fixtures and door handles were rusty. She bought replacements and hired someone to install them. She had expected appliances to break down because of the frequent switchovers from electricity supply to generator but hadn't anticipated that the air in Lekki would be so salty and moist that it would corrode just about every metal surface.

To this day, she oversees repairs in the flat, hiring one incompetent artisan after another and vowing to withhold their final payments until they finish their work properly. They never arrive on time and are sometimes weeks late. They cheat her by inflating their invoices and buying secondhand parts. They call her "Mummy" to appease her and take it personally when she points out that she's not their mother but their client. She has given up confronting them because whenever she does they look stupefied. She is hoping that, if nothing else, the reviews section on Home Pro will finally make everyone in their industry sit up, instead of sending happy new month greetings by WhatsApp to maintain good business relationships.

"Are you still at it?" she asks Yimika, who is now busy scrolling on her phone.

"Almost finished," Yimika says.

"Good," Enitan says. "I need your advice, please."

Yimika nods distractedly. "Sure."

Enitan gets up and plods to the kitchen. There, she opens a door of the double fridge and surveys her neat piles of plastic food packs. She still won't cook if she can help it. She orders meals in bulk from Bakare Bukka, a chain of buffet restaurants started by her childhood friend Sheri, who is now based in Abuja and visits Lagos every so often. Their food is consistently good, and tonight Enitan chooses fried rice and barbecue catfish and heats them up in the microwave.

As she eats at the dining table, she tells Yimika about her visit to the prison.

"I felt like a complete fraud."

Indigene

"That's a little extreme."

"It's true, though."

"You still went there."

"Yeah..."

"See? So you *are* making a difference."

Enitan momentarily cups her mouth. "Why does everyone keep using meaningless American expressions?"

She is baffled by the Americanization of Nigeria in general. She speaks to junior lawyers who have never lived in the United States, yet they exaggerate their Rs and end their sentences like questions. She turns on her car radio and presenters chatter in African American slang. She gets promotional messages from her bank about Thanksgiving and Black Friday.

"Relax, Mum," Yimika says. "My brain's just fried."

"Seriously," Enitan says. "I'm getting tired of it and that Isioma woman is full of them. She's copying me, you know."

"Uh, are you like two years old or something?"

"She *is* a copycat."

"Oh, grow up."

They sometimes bicker like this. Attacks on each other's generations are the most common. Rather than use terms like millennial and Gen Z that don't quite fit, Enitan refers to the mass media they consumed in their formative years. Her father is a Radio, she is a TV—black-and-white, as opposed to color—and Yimika is an Internet, somewhere on the spectrum between Myspace and TikTok. Yimika thinks TVs like Enitan failed Nigeria by not being politically active. "You guys did nothing," Yimika once said. "That's why the country is such a mess." Enitan thinks Internets are delusional. "What about you lot, who believe that typing hashtags makes you warriors?" she countered.

They've had some enlightening discussions, such as the one about identities Enitan never had to consider when she was growing up. "Why am I a cis woman?" she asked. "Please tell me." Yimika said, "If you don't know by now, that's on you." Enitan, in trying to educate herself, picked up words that Yimika threw at her, like inclusivity and intersectionality.

They've had painful conversations as well—for instance, the one about Yimika's breakup with her boyfriend last year. He and Yimika had studied electronic and information engineering at Imperial College London. He was an unlikely Yoruba demon, having been born and raised in England, yet he gave Yimika the old "It's not you, it's me." Yimika made a video call home and ended up in tears. So did Enitan afterward, because she'd never seen her daughter's eyes that puffy and red, and couldn't convince her the stupid boy wasn't worth crying over.

Because of Enitan's tendency to overreact when it comes to her daughter's relationships, Yimika is reluctant to have conversations of that nature with her. Enitan has learned to wait for Yimika to initiate them. Yimika can also be defensive about her father, so Enitan doesn't criticize him in her presence. She looks at it this way: Niyi is sixty-five and his son from his first marriage is forty-one. They were estranged for years because his son's mother came between them. Besides, even though Niyi has been through two divorces, he is not from a divorced family, as Enitan is, and may not understand the family dynamics from Yimika's point of view. His mother, in spite of his father's domineering ways, stayed married to the man until his death. Enitan isn't sure which of her parents initiated their separation, but she doesn't want to repeat the mistakes they made after their divorce.

She would never use Yimika to settle scores and tries her

best to be civil to Niyi these days. He, too, has become less hostile over the years. Now on his third marriage, he does legal work for an oil company and lives on Banana Island. He has acquired a big man swagger—and an obligatory karma bead bracelet to go with it. Whenever they meet, they greet each other with sideways hugs. His wife, Demi, is always pleasant. She was widowed young when her husband got killed in a car crash, and raised three sons while running her furniture shop. Enitan credits her with Niyi's turnaround.

This was a man who accused her of endangering their unborn child's life when she got detained, and wouldn't speak to her for a whole trimester, to pressure her to stop making further press statements about her father. These days, he encourages Yimika to travel anywhere in the world on her own, for the experience, and says there's nothing wrong with her staying out in Lagos till the early hours of the morning because she is young and entitled to have fun. If Enitan brings up the issue of safety, he accuses her of being overprotective. His tactic works. She doesn't know how she copes with Yimika constantly siding with him while opposing her on almost every issue.

She and Yimika have recently come to an understanding about their living arrangements. They no longer have house help, which is an added source of conflict between them.

In September last year, Enitan had to sack Bright, who burnt a sofa in the living room while ironing on it and almost caused a fire. Bright denied she couldn't be bothered to set up the ironing board and said the devil led her astray. In December, Enitan then had to let go of her driver, Julius, when it became obvious from his erratic steering and dilated pupils that he was abusing drugs. Ladi made the diagnosis just by looking at him. He had several patients who were addicted to opioids and amphetamines. Of course Julius said he wasn't, so Ladi couldn't help him.

Enitan now uses a housecleaning service that Ladi told her about. Two men come in on Sunday mornings, do their work and leave by midday. She takes her major laundry to a dry cleaner down the road. She still hasn't found anyone to replace Julius, but Ladi's driver, Abel, washes her cars once a week to make extra money. She has the Highlander she used today and a RAV4, which she sets aside for Yimika. Yimika has promised to return from her outings around midnight. She, however, doesn't want to hear Enitan's warnings about cultists who kidnap young women and use their body parts for juju rituals, every time she leaves home. She can't see the benefit of being tidy either, but says she will put more effort into keeping the flat clean.

Enitan will take what she can get. Despite their arguments about each other's generation, she has followed the progress of Yimika's friends and is impressed with nearly all of them. Whether they were educated in Nigeria or overseas, or here and there as Yimika was, they are hardworking and enterprising. They search and move globally for jobs. Some of them, however, are still living at home with their parents and doing nothing but wanting, and they usually want to be creatives or gatekeepers of creatives.

A school friend of Yimika's, whose stage name was Banx, wanted to be a recording artist. Banx apparently didn't have enough talent, but that didn't deter his parents. They made a phone call to their friend, the chairman of a record label, on his behalf. Banx didn't get a deal. He then said he wanted to be a DJ, so his parents bought him the necessary equipment. He got hired for a couple of gigs before turning his attention to branding himself on Instagram and Twitter. His parents paid for his PR, but he became so obsessed with wanting to trend and stay relevant online that he eventually became depressed. Yimika said it could have happened to any of her friends.

No one makes light of mental health anymore. No one jokes about the likelihood of getting disowned for announcing they want to be artists either, and if Internets think they're special and outspoken, they rarely attribute it to how TVs raised them.

Enitan wouldn't dare point a finger at other parents for ruining their children. She has told Yimika before, "You're spoiled," and has admitted to her, "I spoiled you." At the same time, she also observed parents of Yimika's friends being shockingly obliging with their children, including parents who had sense physically beaten into them and believed it worked. She doesn't know if they are imitating oyinbos or hoping their kids will become the next Afropop stars or tech billionaires, but their permissive approach hasn't always worked in their favor. She isn't proud of her mothering skills, but is nonetheless thankful she didn't spoil Yimika too much.

On the subject of Indigene, Yimika thinks Enitan should stop visiting them if she doesn't see the point and suggests she send them her care packages on a regular basis instead. Enitan says that would make her no different from the ladies who launch.

Yimika raises her hand. "Why are you even comparing yourself to them?"

"It's not about them," Enitan says. "It's about having character. Now there's an expression we don't hear enough anymore. You can't just hop on causes to make you look good. You can't just give up on a project because you don't see the point of it. In my time, having character was important."

"Look where that got us."

"How's living your best life working out?"

"Living an authentic one might."

"There's no such thing, darling."

"Okay, Mum."

Enitan makes a confused face. Usually, Yimika pesters her with questions about Indigenes out of concern: "How were they?" "What did they say?" Her stance tonight is surprising, but perhaps she is assessing the matter from a professional standpoint.

She appreciates her daughter's advice. She trusts her judgement as well, perhaps more than she should, but this is the hardest decision she's made since her divorce. Continuing as she has with Indigene will be hard. Giving up will be harder still, so before she decides what to do, she will speak to Ladi when she sees him later tonight, and to her father, when she visits him tomorrow afternoon. She might even ask Sheri's opinion when they next speak on the phone.

"Thanks, Yimz," she says. "I forgive you."

"I forgive you, too, Mum."

Forgiveness substitutes for love. It began as a joke after an argument and soon became their routine.

Yimika is out with her girlfriends when Ladi shows up at the flat. He wants to have dinner at a restaurant, as they normally would on a Saturday evening, but Enitan would rather stay at home. She is still preoccupied with Indigene and is in the clothes she's worn all day. He looks ready to go in his neatly ironed navy tunic and trousers. Sixty-two, with a dependable manner, he is a little taller than Enitan and sports a gray moustache and beard. She often teases him that he has an unimpressed resting face, which he says is an accurate reflection of his state of mind. He, too, has become farsighted with age, but his glasses are rectangular while hers are oval. They stand at opposite ends of the dining table and negotiate what to do next.

"Why don't you just stay here and have some Bakare Bukka?" she asks.

"No," he says. "I'm tired of Bakare Bukka. Every time I come here, it's Bakare Bukka."

Enitan laughs. "I've already eaten!"

"So sit and watch me eat."

"That's all I ever do."

He rarely makes conversation while he eats. She does the talking and he listens.

"Come on," he says, "let's get out of here before the restaurants close."

"I haven't had a shower!"

"You don't need one."

Enitan folds her arms. "I'm not going anywhere until I've had one and changed."

Ladi is silent for a moment, then he gestures. "Oya. Hurry up, then."

She beckons to him so they can continue their conversation in her bedroom.

He frowns. "Aren't we breaking the rules?"

"What rules?" she asks. "Follow me, my friend, and stop pretending you're a virgin."

He gives her a puzzled look she always finds appealing, even though it's meant to suggest he is questioning her sanity. They have one rule only. Neither of them can sleep over when the other's child or children are around. His son, Damola, and his daughter, Adeola, are now married, so the rule applies to him alone, but they haven't spent a weekend together since Yimika has been home.

Enitan's bedroom has a queen-sized bed that faces built-in cupboards and two windows with dreadful views of neighboring blocks, so the wall opposite them, where the door is, has oil paintings that please her—an old man smoking a pipe and a young girl crouching. Ladi deftly lowers himself onto her bed while supporting himself with his arm. He has a bad knee he's loath to complain about. A karate black belt, he participated in competitive sparring in medical school. Now, all he does for sport is play golf on Sundays.

As she gives him an account of her visit to the prison, she takes off her clothes and walks to her bathroom naked. There, she sits on the toilet and pees with the door open, then she waits a few seconds for her bladder to decide if it's empty or not.

When she first noticed this symptom, she got scared that she would soon start wetting herself if she sneezed or coughed too hard. Her gynecologist explained that pelvic floor muscles weakened with age and recommended she did Kegel exercises to strengthen them. Ladi later advised her to try and make the best use of them before they atrophied.

She continues talking to him as she steps into her shower with an unflattering white cap on her head and takes her exfoliating glove from the soap dish. She puts it on and turns around, relishing how the warm water hits her back. The pressure pump she had installed still works well, but the pipes make such a noise she can't hear Ladi clearly.

"Why did you start Indigene in the first place?" he asks from her bedroom.

Indigene

"What?"

He is not one to raise his voice, but he makes an effort. "What was your reason for starting Indigene?"

Enitan begins to wash her face with the glove, making gentle circular motions, and shuts her eyes. The blackness is so opaque she can see her conscience. "Guilt!"

"That's no reason to start anything."

"Speak louder! I can't hear you!"

"Guilt isn't a good reason to start anything!"

"I know! But stopping won't change how I feel!"

"Why not?"

He is dismissive of guilt, regret or any such emotions that can be avoided by making sensible decisions. Enitan thinks carefully about what to say as her shower glass steams up.

"I can't unsee what I've seen!"

Ladi is silent for a moment, which means he agrees with her.

"You have to take things easy! Life isn't this hard!"

"Of course it is! What are you saying?"

"Okay, try dealing with death, then."

"What?"

"Try dealing with death instead!"

Enitan scrubs the back of her neck. He is annoyingly pragmatic. He doesn't disclose his patients' identities, but has mentioned that a few have died simply because they were previously misdiagnosed or prescribed the wrong medication.

Two Christmases ago, her tailor, John, had a stroke and was fortunate enough to be rushed to Lagos State University Teaching Hospital by his neighbor, an Uber driver. She and Ladi went there to see him, and it gave her a little more insight into what doctors dealt with. She hadn't stepped inside a public hospital since she was a child, and was surprised that this one appeared clean and well organized. John was in the medical emergency department, which had a patient care manifesto, holiday decorations and a wall-mounted television. Oddly enough, the film *Die Hard* was on. The ward was full of patients in varying stages of consciousness, some with oxygen tubes up their noses. John could barely keep his eyes open, and she regretted the times she'd criticized him for his lateness, uneven seams and invoice padding. Ladi spoke to the neurology resident about his progress and found out that John had been taking antibiotics instead of blood thinners, because his doctor thought he had pneumonia.

John eventually recovered and managed to pay his hospital bills, with help from her and other clients, but only last week Ladi lost a patient who went to a private hospital for an endoscopy and ended up suffocating from a lung aspiration. He said the anesthesiologist and nurses hadn't done whatever was required to make sure his patient had an empty stomach.

He's been following news reports about the novel coronavirus, which Enitan assumed would be locally controlled, until he reminded her of the Ebola epidemic in 2014. He has good reason to be pragmatic, but he can't possibly compare his dilemmas to hers.

"Why are you bringing up death?" she asks. "It trivializes everything!"

"Finish your shower first!" he says. "We can't keep shouting like this!"

She turns towards the showerhead and rinses her face and neck. The water from the treatment plant is not safe to drink, so she keeps her mouth shut as she opens her eyes.

Indigene

Ladi graduated from the College of Medicine, University of Lagos, and completed his house job at Lagos University Teaching Hospital, after which he worked at his father's clinic during his National Youth Service. A year later, he took off to England, where he sat and passed the Professional and Linguistic Assessments Board test but couldn't find positions in internal medicine, the field he wanted to specialize in. He did temporary jobs as a locum doctor for the National Health Service until he got his first rotation and was considering taking the United States Medical Licensing Examination and moving to America when his father died from a heart seizure. Rather than doing that, he returned to Lagos.

Everyone said he was mad—his friends, his colleagues, his brother, an accountant, and his sister, a dentist, both of whom were in London with him. His late mother, a retired nurse, was ready to close the clinic and sell it, but he, the last-born in his family, convinced her not to and began to run the place. Using the building as collateral and his connection with a former classmate, he got a bank loan and bought land in Lekki when it was undeveloped. Several years later, he sold the land and made enough profit to repay the loan and build his own clinic. His mother followed her wish and he retained his father's staff.

His speculative investment was more successful than his marriage. While he was being careful with money, his ex-wife, Fadeke, a pharmacist, felt they deserved a better lifestyle. A gregarious woman who couldn't turn down an invitation to a party, she spent hundreds of thousands of naira on aṣọ ẹbi. They argued over her excesses and in the end decided to part ways. A few years after their separation, she started seeing a divorced banker and soon married him.

Enitan was inclined to take Fadeke's side. A woman like her would be required to keep a job and take care of her home and family. She would also be expected to tolerate her husband's affairs and her interfering in-laws. All she would be allowed to ask for in return was that her husband handled their household bills, giving her the freedom to spend what she earned as she pleased. Why begrudge her a little aṣọ ẹbi? she asked Ladi, who took her question literally. He said their divorce wasn't over aṣọ ẹbi; they just had different priorities.

It was a point in his favor that he didn't run Fadeke down. He and Enitan have been together for over twenty years and neither of them wants to remarry. He once said he loved her enough to go through with it, and she immediately said she loved him enough to spare him. She is perfectly happy to look forward to seeing him for the rest of her life. They speak every day, confide in and support each other, and meet up when they want. What else does she need at this stage in her life?

Before he came along, she'd had ridiculously awful dates, her last one with a telecoms chairman who told her gray hair made her look like a grandmother and suggested she wear wigs. She never imagined she would meet a man who would put up with her lack of desire to cook, but she walked into a dinner party and there Ladi was. They talked, and she was taken by the way he listened as if what she rambled on about was of consequence to him. She wasn't the type of woman to settle for the first man who gave her attention, but hadn't anticipated the loneliness that would accompany her way of thinking. All Ladi did was mention he could cook and she hugged him.

He cooked for her once. The first time she stayed at his place. He made an omelet the next morning—chopped the tomatoes and

Indigene

onions with precision, cracked the eggs with sharp taps, folded the omelet without breaking it and, when he was through, sliced it down the middle for them to share. After that, he left meals to his cook, Mama Titi, who was thankfully territorial in his kitchen.

Her shower over, Enitan emerges from her bathroom with her cap off and a towel wrapped around her body, and stops before Ladi.

"What I'm saying is," he explains, "I don't have free clinics because I feel guilty. You have to enjoy what you do."

"No one enjoys visiting prisoners."

"Okay. Do it because you want to."

"No one wants to visit anyone in prison."

"Fine, but if you can't handle it, it's time to stop."

He is like this with his patients. He won't mollycoddle them. He tells them to give up smoking, reduce their sugar intake, whatever they need to do to get or stay healthy. But everybody she knows has their way of compensating. She has her prison visits and he has his free clinics. How much does he enjoy giving prostate exams anyway?

"Actually, it's not guilt," she says.

"What is it, then?" he asks.

"The Naija condition."

"Which is?"

She hesitates because she doesn't want to sound silly or self-righteous. "What's that quote again? 'We can't be free if we're not all free'?"

Ladi considers this as if it is an original thought. "You'd better not give up, then."

"Wahala," she says, and heads for her dressing table, where her toiletries are neatly arranged.

43

"Where are we going?" he asks, watching her.

"You tell me. You're the one who wants to eat out."

"I'm too hungry to think."

"Okay, love. We'll go in your car and talk about it on our way."

She is consistent with her term of endearment for him. Her daughter is darling, dearest, sweetheart, whatever she feels like calling her, but he is always love.

The next day Enitan visits her father as planned and finds him drinking wine and listening to Ebenezer Obey. This is the most religious he gets on Sundays. Obey's songs are replete with Christian lyrics, and wine, perhaps, allows him to meditate after lunch.

"Ẹku joko," she says, settling into the chair next to his.

"A dupẹ," he replies.

Lean, with stark white hair, he sits up as if he's about to preside over an office meeting. He won't be caught slumping or doddering, not even by Enitan. He is too proud for that. Today he is in his television chair, where he watches local and international news channels and grumbles about world politics. His preferred one is on the veranda, which has a calming view of his garden and Lagos lagoon.

His sitting room has been updated over the years. Gone are the wall clocks and other corporate gifts with logos. The carved calabashes, beaded masks and ayo board remain, but the sofa set in curvy mahogany that gave the room an old-fashioned appearance has been replaced with an angular one in dark-stained wood, following gentle persuasion by Enitan and much resistance from him. He still has his collections of reel-to-reel tapes, records, cartridges and cassettes. She bought him a Bluetooth speaker, which is paired to his iPhone, on which Yimika downloaded

Indigene

favorite songs and classified them into sections for Sunny Adé, Ray Charles, Maria Callas, Dave Brubeck and the rest. Yimika humored him when he said life was easier with rotary phones, five-digit numbers and operators who connected trunk calls.

Never alone at home, his current crew is out of sight, but on standby if he needs them—Bassey, the cook and cleaner, who opened the front door for Enitan; Mr. Disu, the driver; Mr. Mashood, the gardener; and Emmanuel, the gateman, who also manages the electricity generator. Her father deliberately chooses to surround himself with middle-aged men who are content to have an undemanding boss. He has little tolerance for young men, who might not follow instructions, or women, who are liable to get upset if he corrects them. Mr. Disu doesn't seem to mind him being a perpetual backseat driver. Enitan has likened riding in a car with them to watching *Driving Miss Daisy*.

She slips into their pattern of listening to music and talking at intervals.

"How's Yimika?" her father asks.

"She's fine," Enitan says. "She's at home."

Yimika visits him in her own time, and Enitan prefers it that way, so they don't delay or rush each other.

"We've been talking about her business plan," her father says. "I think it's an excellent one."

Enitan shakes her head. "Please don't encourage her. She doesn't know how to run a business here."

Her father eyes her as though she's putting Yimika down. "What do you mean?"

"She needs more work experience."

"Ehen? It's a start-up and she works for one."

"A lot of them fail."

He wants Yimika to come home for good, which is understandable. Enitan's half-brother, Debayo, a pathologist in England, plans to retire there with his wife, Toyosi, a solicitor. Their twin sons, Ayo and Ola, have declared themselves Black British and have no intention of returning to Nigeria. Yimika is more inclined to say she is a Nigerian who works in London. She got her UK right of abode through Niyi, who was born in England but hasn't lived there since he and his parents returned to Nigeria in the late 1950s. Yimika herself hasn't lived in Lagos in years but is toying with the idea because she enjoys the social scene and fears that London will change for the worse after Brexit. Enitan is wary of her plan to set up a business, only because Taiwo and Associates' client list is full of people who have been bankrupted in the course of doing that.

The business in question is plastic recycling. Yimika is appalled by the pollution she sees in Lekki and other parts of Lagos and would like to be part of the limited effort to clean up the environment. Enitan is willing to admit that she could do without the daily spectacle of plastic bottles, Styrofoam cups and cellophane wraps that clog up gutters and canals in Lekki. But she recognizes why environmental concerns aren't on top of the list of government priorities in a place where people beg for money at every traffic light.

She pointed this out to Yimika, who enthused about the possibility of building a sustainable business ecosystem. Overwhelmed by the thought of buying a recycling plant and shipping it over, Enitan told her to speak to Niyi about getting a job as an environmentalist in the oil company he represented instead. "I would never work for a fossil fuel company," Yimika protested.

Indigene

"Well," Enitan said, "that's how your father was able to pay for your education." She suggested that Yimika's best bet with plastic recycling in Lagos would be to set up an NGO and look for foreign donors who wanted to save the world and had plenty of funds to give desperate Africans. Yimika called her a hater but saw no problem in approaching her fossil fuel father to ask if he would invest in the business. Not surprisingly, he agreed to.

"What about Ladi?" her father asks.

"He's okay," Enitan says. "I saw him yesterday."

"I haven't heard from him in a while."

"He says I should greet you."

Her father merely nods. He no longer drops hints that they should get married, but continues to show his disapproval for their common law spouse status, despite his own. Ladi sometimes visits him alone and brings a bottle of wine.

"Are you hearing from Auntie?" she asks.

Her father nods again. "We spoke earlier today."

"That's good. When is she coming back?"

"Early next month, she says."

Her father's longtime companion, Auntie Simi, is a widow and retired lawyer in her late seventies. A kind and patient woman, she is spending time with her daughter and grandchildren in Atlanta. Enitan has met her family and is relieved she is old enough to be called Auntie. She's heard enough stories about her father's peers carrying on with women half their age and burdening them with geriatric chores.

Committed to staying fit and healthy, her father sticks to a daily regimen. He gets up at seven in the mornings and does stretches before walking around his yard several times. He watches his news programs at intervals and by nine o'clock he's in bed. He is the last of three Nigerian musketeers at Cambridge, having survived his college mates Uncle Alex, who was killed during the civil war, and Uncle Fatai, who died a few years ago after a protracted battle with colon cancer. He is, as he often assures Enitan, determined to be around for a long time.

She asks his advice about Indigene, and after a pause he says, "To whom much is given, of them much is required."

It isn't unusual for him to be brief. He's given to making statements like "Begin as you mean to continue" and "Character is important." She might borrow such lines while speaking to Yimika but, like old wives' tales, she can't rely on them. What if someone starts off wrongly? Who is character important to anyway, except those who possess it?

Her father is generous the way wealthy Nigerian elders are. He considers it a call of duty to bankroll relatives and donate money to causes. He's even had a school built in his hometown, which of course has his name on it, yet he won't pay his house help more than competitive salary rates. Enitan wonders if he was referring to himself or to God in bringing up how much she's been given. She is, after all, a partner in the law firm he started. Because of this, she was able to buy her place in Lekki and a two-bedroom flat in North-West London. She doubts her father believes that God is responsible for her net worth, but she thanks him for his advice with a courteous nod and "Ẹse."

Greeting her father in Yoruba is her way of showing him affection. She also thinks he deserves it, with the number of casual hellos he gets from his grandkids. She doesn't tell him she loves him or vice versa. He would probably find it childish of her to expect that, but he willingly exchanges love-yous with Yimika and the twins and accepts their pet name for him—Gramps.

Enitan never thought she'd see the day her father, a whole Yoruba man, who left his hometown in Kwara State to attend Cambridge University and called England the Heart of Darkness, on account of the indignities he suffered there, would settle for his culturally confused grandchildren saying, "Hello, Gramps" and "Love you, Gramps," but he does.

Growing up with him, she never felt unloved, but she often felt culpable for family circumstances. Her younger brother, Jola, was born with sickle cell anemia and was in and out of hospital until he died. Her parents argued nonstop. Her father was hardly ever at home. Her late mother, Arin, joined a white-gown church and took her there every Sunday. The priest at her mother's church singled her out for a spiritual cleansing. She got scared and told her father, who stopped her mother from taking her there again. He was put off by her mother's religiosity and cited the church incident as proof of child endangerment to gain custody of Enitan. Enitan blamed herself for telling.

When she was old enough to piece together what had happened, she distanced herself from her mother. She couldn't understand how a parent could leave his or her child open to being stigmatized and possibly molested over any religious belief. Then she found out about Debayo, her father's son by another woman, and blamed her father until she came to terms with the fact that her family wasn't unusual. Her mother wouldn't be the first to turn to the church in a bad marriage. Her father wouldn't be the first to appear heroic until he revealed his flaws. Besides, family complications occurred long before they were labeled as separations and divorces, and siblings were identified as half-this and step-that. She stopped judging her parents in her late twenties when she finally acknowledged that it was no longer convenient to do so.

Her father points at a folded newspaper on the side table between them. "Take a look at this."

Enitan opens it up and sees a headline that states, "Pa Taiwo on Restructuring."

"You're still on the matter?" she asks.

He ignores her taunt. "Just read it."

Enitan skims through the article. Her father is officially a Pa, which puts him on a short list of octogenarians whose political opinions are still sought-after by the press, even though they have no influence over the direction Nigeria is heading. But Pa Taiwo will not be condescended to and has become more obstinate with age.

He is furious with President Buhari, who professes not to know what restructuring entails or how to implement it. Most Nigerians don't either, in Enitan's assessment. To her father, restructuring is a regionally decentralized system of government, which he calls true federalism in the article. Enitan's view is that politicians will continue to thrive and dominate with or without restructuring. The evidence, she would say, is obvious in the way that governors are freely able to run down their states, and in how the legislature succeeded in getting executive approval for the highest salary and benefits packages in Nigeria for themselves and other elected officials.

She presumes her father wrote the article because he gets bored, now that he's retired from practicing law, but she doesn't understand why he has taken it upon himself to defend the constitution singlehandedly. He is not a member of Afenifere, who are major proponents of restructuring, because he doesn't

Indigene

trust groups that are founded on ethnic affiliations, Yoruba or otherwise. He maintains he was never part of the pro-democracy movement of the 1990s, which included groups like the Campaign for Democracy and the National Democratic Coalition, and was merely representing his client, Peter Mukoro, the late journalist. Like Mukoro, so many activists who escaped being killed during the movement ended up dying from illnesses. Others became politicians after Nigeria's return to democracy and some inevitably enriched themselves through fraudulent means, to her father's disapproval.

Enitan finds his way of engaging in national politics futile. She turned sixty earlier this month, as Nigeria will, with much festivity, in October. All she did was go out for dinner with Yimika, Ladi and her father. She'd never seen why she had to celebrate round-number birthdays more than others. Nor had she ever considered announcing them in newspapers and magazines, along with a photo spread and biography, as was the wont in Lagos society. Being sixty made her more mindful of her duties, personal, professional and civic, but publicly criticizing leaders who clearly didn't care about Nigeria wasn't one of them. Military rulers showed blatant disregard for the constitution by suspending it at will, and civilian presidents barely pretend to respect it.

Discussing the problems of Nigeria has become a national daily rite, but solution offerings are rare, so Enitan appreciates her father's continued efforts. He thinks the caliber of Nigerian presidents worsens with each election. She thinks Nigeria itself is deteriorating and presidents to date have been too self-interested and preoccupied with party politics to do anything about it. She has developed a sense of complacency about how the country is run because she has seen that Buhari is incapable of overseeing the civil service and other institutions, let alone figuring out how to improve them. She doesn't blame him for his ignorance or incompetence. It is not his fault.

The man came to power after he overthrew President Shagari's administration in a coup d'état in 1983. Decree 2, under which persons suspected of acts prejudicial to the state were detained indefinitely, was passed during his regime. This and his so-called War Against Indiscipline were legacies of his term as head of state. He then ran for president in 2003, 2007 and 2011 until he was elected in 2015. He promised to clamp down on corruption, his professed pet peeve, but never delivered. He hardly said a word about the economy, so it was no wonder that the national debt was out of control and poverty was widespread. He did make a few half-hearted announcements about tackling insecurity, but couldn't stop Boko Haram, let alone the armed Fulani herdsmen who wreaked havoc on the communities they raided. Buhari couldn't even bring back the remaining Chibok girls, yet Nigerians saw fit to re-elect him in 2019.

Nigeria, as far as Enitan is concerned, is old enough to know better, and Nigerians are still complaining about no water, no light in 2020, so unless Buhari is able to resolve these two basic longstanding problems, she doesn't want to hear him talk about restructuring.

"You think he'll bother to read it?" she asks, when she comes to the end of the article.

"I didn't write it for him," her father says.

Enitan folds the newspaper and returns it to the table. Restructuring is a Radio concern, as the environment will be to a generation yet to be born. TVs are doing what they can to get by, and Internets are trying to make it or get out of the country—blow or japa—by any means.

She says nothing more about the article and instead gives her father an update on what happened at work the week before. This usually cheers him up.

Her father's retirement was both welcome and unnerving for her. She was used to having him around as an advisor and confidant at Taiwo and Associates, but it was also high time her fellow partners, Dagogo and Alabi, stopped treating her like the boss's daughter.

She threw her father a farewell party at the office and told him about it in advance because he didn't like surprises. He made it clear that he wasn't interested in having a bigger event, even as Dagogo and Alabi took issue with her for respecting his wishes. Dagogo said a simple get-together was beneath a man of her father's stature, and Alabi said her father had no choice but to accept a full-scale owambẹ that would shut down the whole of Lagos. Enitan asked if they were prepared to make a contribution to said bash, and predictably that was the last she heard about it.

She was nervous about planning the party, but it went well in the end. Former employees like Peace, her father's one-time secretary, who had constantly complained about her General Body Weakness, turned up. So did Mrs. Kazeem, otherwise known as Mama Ibeji, who for many years was the firm's company secretary. It was lovely to see them again and remember them as they were, the former unintentionally funny and the latter deliberately strict.

Taiwo and Associates has since relocated to Military Street in Onikan. Its proximity to bridges that connect Lagos Island

and mainland makes commuting a little easier for employees, but they arrive early and leave late to avoid traffic or to find parking spaces. The firm is on the top floor of an office block, and below it are three floors occupied by other businesses. On the ground floor is Small Chops, a cafeteria where employees have lunch at a discount. Apart from Enitan and her fellow partners, the firm has four senior associates and eight junior associates, which narrowly qualifies it as mid-sized in Lagos. Employees tend to go on leave around Christmas and New Year, because business slows down, but they are back at work now.

On Monday morning, Enitan buys akara and pineapple juice from Small Chops and heads upstairs for a meeting with Dagogo and Alabi. She is able to finish her breakfast at her desk and clean up before they walk in. Her office is smaller than theirs, but has glass sliding doors that extend to a balcony on which she has potted plants such as mother-in-law's tongue and queen of the night. Rather than use her air conditioner, she keeps the doors open to get fresh air. From her desk, she has a view of Lagos harbor, the National Museum, the Musical Society of Nigeria center and J. K. Randle Memorial Hall, which is currently being converted to a center for Yoruba culture and history.

Today, she is in her work uniform, a black skirt suit and white blouse. Dagogo and Alabi are in theirs—black suits, white shirts and dark ties. She calls them "sir" because they are in their late sixties and they, in turn, call her "Madam Enitan." She's always been fond of them and has become more tolerant of their ways, enough to ignore chauvinistic digs that may have infuriated her in her twenties. Alabi is less mercurial than he was when she joined the firm and has developed a lovable-uncle

Indigene

paunch. Dagogo is still easygoing and wears playful socks that his daughter gifts him. They are both Senior Advocates of Nigeria, which helps the firm's profile. Enitan, like her father, never applied for the title and agrees with his opinion that it is exclusionary.

Following their greetings and inquiries about weekend activities, Dagogo and Alabi sit in chairs across from hers, blocking her view.

"Where are we on the training of juniors?" Alabi asks.

"I'm where I was last year," Enitan says.

"I see," Alabi says, lowering his gaze.

Dagogo characteristically twiddles his thumbs. "What does Baba say?"

Before they became partners, Dagogo and Alabi privately referred to her father, Bandele Sunday, as "BS," after his initials.

"He agrees with me," Enitan says.

"Maybe we should reconsider?" Dagogo asks, glancing at Alabi.

Alabi sways in his usual self-important manner. "Um . . . we can try it this year and see how it goes."

"Thank you, sirs," Enitan says. "I found a consultancy online. They have workshops in April and June this year. I'll send you a link to their website later."

Dagogo and Alabi are opposed to spending more on training junior associates because of their high turnover rate. They stay for a few years and leave for bigger firms once they have opportunities. Enitan believes the firm will benefit from training them regardless. For as long as she can remember, it has been difficult to recruit newly qualified lawyers who write well. State university graduates can barely construct their application letters, and even private university graduates need a lot of editorial help. The consultancy is in Ikeja and provides writing courses on legal analyses, opinions and briefs. Senior associates travel overseas for training courses to keep up in their areas of expertise. That won't change because they have more loyalty to the firm.

A year ago, Dagogo and Alabi were shocked when a senior associate, Ifueko, resigned. Ifueko graduated with first class honors from the Nigerian Law School. She was great with clients, brilliant at writing briefs and fierce in court. Enitan thought she ought to be made a partner, but Dagogo and Alabi were against the idea, asking "How can?" and "For where?" They both felt that Ifueko hadn't paid her dues, but neither of them had a clue that Enitan was behind her father's decision to make them partners.

She told her father outright that it was unfair, unwise and unrealistic to expect them to continue to work for the firm without sharing in the profits. He said he didn't start Taiwo and Associates to leave it to strangers. She said his approach was outdated and cited cases in which siblings had sued each other over their interests in family firms. He said the cases were irrelevant unless she had intentions of suing herself. Enitan kept pushing him. He'd qualified at a time when lawyers were so few they were guaranteed social mobility. In her time, lawyers weren't even guaranteed a job, and if they were employed, they needed side hustles to pay their bills.

To this day, Enitan regrets not approaching her father to weigh in on the matter of Ifueko. She was worried that bypassing Dagogo and Alabi would cause friction. Now, she is relieved that Ifueko isn't around to remind her of her omission.

After the meeting, Muyiwa, a senior associate, comes to her

office to report on his progress with clients' perfection of title documents. Muyiwa is lanky and his suits hang on him, but his unassuming appearance gives him an advantage in court and endears him to his clients and colleagues.

"Good morning, ma," he says, bowing slightly as he stands before her.

"Morning, Muyiwa," she says. "How was your weekend?"

"Fine thank you, ma."

Employees show courtesies to their seniors in the office. Dagogo wouldn't mind if everyone went by their first names, but Alabi is opposed to a casual work culture. He grew up groveling to his elders, and now that he's one, wouldn't appreciate a change of rules. Enitan's father raised her to regard Yoruba civilities as a mark of refinement. His grandchildren aside, if people don't address each other accordingly, he ascribes it to a lack of home training. Enitan has reservations about this, but her stance is that if junior associates are cosmopolitan enough to observe foreign customs when they travel overseas, they can jolly well follow customs at home.

"Any updates from your bank about your money?" she asks Muyiwa.

He smiles as he does when he's nervous. "I can't get it back."

"Why not?"

"They say I have no proof I was robbed."

"Goodness," Enitan says, thinking, Damn.

Muyiwa shares a flat in Lekki Phase Two with friends. In December, they were returning from a lounge in his car at night when he was stopped by the Special Anti-Robbery Squad, who ordered him to drive to the nearest ATM, where he had to withdraw money from his account and hand it over.

Enitan has never encountered SARS policemen, who won't hesitate to shoot and kill, but when she was Muyiwa's age, regular policemen harassed her for money at checkpoints and she had to be careful about how she responded because they were armed. Most recently, she was pulled over by an officer who, after checking the validity of her driver's license, insurance certificate and road worthiness tag, said it was illegal for her to lower her back seats. She told him there was no such law and he insisted there was, delaying her until his partner ambled over and persuaded him to let her go.

"Not the best way to start the year," she adds.

Muyiwa smiles again. "No, ma."

Enitan makes a doubtful face. "Let's hope it brings us clarity, if nothing else."

The word clarity has been overused of late, by Nigerian television and newspaper pundits, in their deliberations on the state of the nation, but it best describes what she is looking for.

Enitan doesn't speak to Sheri until early February, during a four-day petrol shortage that Sheri calls her to complain about. They usually keep in touch with each other by phone, preferring that to exchanging texts or WhatsApp messages.

"What is all this nonsense?" Sheri asks. "Why are we pretending we're in a normal oil-producing country? We might as well use malu for transport and turn their dung into fuel, at this rate."

Enitan, just as exasperated, is thankful that Abel managed to get her car tank filled. He spent an entire afternoon queuing up on a road leading to a petrol station while she was at work and paid him for his time.

Indigene

Sheri, who has a fleet of cars and team of drivers at her disposal in Abuja, pronounces everyone from the executives of Nigerian National Petroleum Corporation to the oil marketers ole buruku, and when she's through abusing them, shifts her irritation to their conversation about Indigene.

"Why are you always going to prison?" she asks. "What are you looking for there?"

"I beg, I beg," Enitan says. "Don't start on me."

"But it's true. You've been in prison since I've known you."

"Thank you. Just give me an answer, please."

They met when they were eleven-year-olds, and Sheri still thinks she has a right to play senior because she was born two months earlier. The first child in her polygamous family, her siblings can't even utter her name without prefacing it with "Sister."

She lowers her voice like some mafia don. "Send the women food packs every month. I can arrange that for you at a discount and they will prefer it to visits. Trust me."

Sheri believes that good food alleviates every problem, and founded Bakare Bukka on that premise. The chain has branches in shopping centers throughout Lagos Island and mainland. Every day, its employees share buffet leftovers and distribute a proportion to beggars in food packs. This is the Bakares' way of compensating. Sheri and her family own the company. She is Chief Executive Officer; her brother Gani, second-born, is Chief Financial Officer; her sister, Kudi, third-born, is Chief Communications Officer; and Moshood, who comes after Kudi, is Chief Operating Officer.

Their late father was a Lagos chief—and a tycoon, when successful businessmen were so identified. He was called Chief

Bakare, Alhaji Bakare or Engineer Bakare. He met Sheri's mother, an Englishwoman, just after he graduated from university. Her name was Betty and she may have been a chambermaid. She had Sheri out of wedlock and the revelation of her clandestine relationship with a black man caused such an uproar in her family that they were forced to separate.

Sheri was a toddler when her father brought her to Nigeria on the pretext that they were coming on holiday and handed her over to his mother, known as Alhaja. She grew up in Isalẹ Eko believing her own mother had died, and stayed with Alhaja as her father set up house in Ikeja and later moved to Ikoyi with his wives, Mama Gani and Mama Kudi, and her younger siblings. Alhaja made a fortune in the seventies from selling imported lace and other fabrics to Lagos society women, and Sheri learned about the practicalities of running a business while assisting her in her shop. According to her, Alhaja kept her petty cash at home in an aluminum serving bowl with a cover. The same type of bowl she served food in, enamel glazed and flowery patterned. Alhaja entrusted Sheri from a young age to count the money, to make sure it was replenished and balanced. The image alone helped Enitan understand how her friend progressed from Isalẹ Eko princess to big madam.

These days, Sheri stays at her Parkview Estate flat when she's in Lagos, and Enitan stops by on a Sunday afternoon in mid-February before visiting her father. Sheri's building is a six-story gray-and-white block near Parkview Astoria hotel, which she uses as a landmark. In fact her sitting room resembles a hotel lounge. It has an enormous crystal chandelier, a large Persian rug and two long sofas facing each other. On her glass center table is a Chinese porcelain vase, and on her walls are paintings of Yoruba women in full regalia. Sheri herself looks more Hausa in a coral voile caftan, diamond hoop earrings and a wrist full of gold bangles. She has dressed in similar fashion since she went on hajj to Mecca and Enitan, who wears an ankara maxi dress, can't help but tease her.

"Sanu Hajiya," she says.

"Aburo," Sheri says. "Kini nkọ?"

They relax on the sofas and catch up. Sheri, in true Bakare fashion, pesters Enitan to have something to eat and drink, feigning offense as Enitan, who has already had lunch, repeatedly declines. She then asks after Ladi and Yimika, and Enitan tells her Ladi is fine, but worried about the novel coronavirus, which the World Health Organization has named COVID-19. He has already ordered protective equipment for his clinic. Yimika is doing her best to be tidy, which isn't saying much. Her latest assertion is that she doesn't need to clean her shower. The water and soapsuds do the work. Sheri is her godmother, and Enitan would like them to sit down together and talk about the realities of running a business in Lagos, but Yimika refuses to, suspecting it's a ruse to deter her.

"Don't worry," Sheri says. "When she's ready, I'm here."

She is surprisingly mild when it comes to dealing with Internets. It doesn't matter what they get up to. She listens to them calmly and reasons with them, for which she's earned a cool-aunt reputation.

"How's Nasiru?" Enitan asks.

Sheri sighs. "He's all right. He's in Kaduna again. I keep reminding him that he's sixty-six and a grandfather of twelve, but he says he will slow down when I do."

"You'll both be waiting for each other."

Sheri is now the third wife of Nasiru Yakubu, a Hausa businessman who runs a family business in Kaduna. The company was founded by his grandfather, who traded groundnuts. His father manufactured groundnut oil, and Nasiru combines groundnut and other oils to make margarine. He shuttles between Abuja and Kaduna by plane because armed bandits have taken over the expressway.

"He travels too much," Sheri says. "We haven't had a plane crash since the Dana Air one, but he has to be careful."

"He'll be fine," Enitan says, knowing there is no guarantee.

Nasiru went to Kaduna Capital School, graduated from Ahmadu Bello University in Zaria and got his MBA from London Business School. Sheri took a course in managing family companies that he taught at Lagos Business School. She was Muslim, which counted. She was also somewhat traditional, which helped in Nasiru's social circle. He was the kind of Muslim who drank alcohol in private, and Sheri was the sort who hoped that fasting might help her lose weight. She got along well with his other wives, and they each had their section on the family estate. Enitan never went there because the idea of visiting Sheri in a polygamous compound put her off, but Sheri once said that if Enitan thought the Lagos elite were extravagant, she had to see how the northern elite lived.

"What have you decided about Indigene?" Sheri asks.

"Man," Enitan says. "I haven't made up my mind yet."

"Why not?"

Enitan shrugs. "Honestly, I have no idea."

She is decisive at work, but just thinking about Indigene makes her anxious. Perhaps it reminds her of failure. She hasn't given up on a challenge since her marriage.

Indigene

She asks Sheri about Bakare Bukka, sure that there will be family melodrama to entertain her. The Bakares are loyal to each other and observe rules of seniority, but they air grievances openly and on the spot.

Sheri laughs. "Hah? How could I forget? Your people are attacking us on the Internet!"

"Which people?"

"Your feminist people."

"Why?"

"Because they're crazy."

Enitan listens in amusement as Sheri tells her about the interview she gave to an online magazine for its Valentine's Day issue titled "Women We Love," and how a feminist group in Lagos took offense at comments she'd made. She said she owed the success of Bakare Bukka to women who didn't want to cook and being in a polygamous family was her superpower. The group retweeted the interview, questioning whether Sheri was the right role model to inspire Nigerian women. Kudi, who also happened to be a Yoruba movie actress with over a million followers on Twitter, replied that the group couldn't even inspire Nigerian women to join them. That began a back and forth. The group accused Kudi and Sheri of internalized sexism. Kudi called them a bunch of bitches, then Gani, who really ought to have kept out of the matter, tweeted that Kudi should apologize immediately because he was against cruelty to animals. The group virtually lost their minds. They branded Gani a misogynist and called for a boycott of Bakare Bukka.

"It got that serious?" Enitan asks.

Sheri hisses. "Don't mind them. They have nothing better to do."

She thinks feminism is for oyinbo women. To prove her point, she says Yoruba doesn't have words for he and she or him and her. She looks to the genderless ọmọluabi qualities that Alhaja instilled in her to determine what is best practice—work hard, stay humble, show courage and goodwill, tell the truth and respect other people. She defends polygamy on the grounds that most Nigerian civil marriages are shams.

Enitan can't remember the last time anyone associated her with feminists. She was often blamed for inciting rebellion among other wives when she was married to Niyi, but never took that seriously. What was she protesting about anyway? Domestic disputes on their estate, Sunrise. She was merely fed up with hearing about men who had cheated on their wives, and women who worked overtime while doing their best to take care of their children without help from their husbands. Women who considered themselves lucky to be married but wouldn't wish men like their husbands on their daughters. She thought that was sad, yet she also had to ask herself who their husbands were having affairs with and who were most likely to judge them for neglecting their families.

She had a stint in banking when the sector was newly privatized, and it was no secret that several of her colleagues were having extramarital affairs. Some of them were women. One worked in Customer Service and had the most cheerful smile. Her husband barged into the department and split her lip while slapping her around. Another woman who worked in Internal Audit displayed lovely family photos on her desk. Her mother-in-law told anyone who cared to listen that she was a witch and her youngest child was by some other man.

Circumstances like these are no longer rare, and philandering husbands would be lucky to have wives who remain faithful to them. They may even be well advised to take paternity tests if their children don't resemble them. At the same time, Enitan has observed how any woman with a gripe can declare herself a feminist and find her way to online platforms and scour the Internet for comments to take umbrage at.

What qualifies them to be spokeswomen? she wonders. Where are the feminist academics in Nigerian universities to tell her something she doesn't know? Where are the Iyaloja, like Alhaja, who have had experience organizing? All she hears about these days are posturers, most of whom position themselves as leaders.

"Maybe you should issue a press statement," she says.

Sheri looks confused. "For what?"

"To protect your brand or whatever businesses do in situations like this."

Sheri pats her chest. "Me? They don't know who they're dealing with. I've seen them coming. Kudi is the one who has time for them."

Sheri has had dealings with the press, being a former Miss Nigeria, yet she is uncomfortable with social media. She watches Kudi's films and follows her on Facebook, Twitter and Instagram, but has in the past fallen out with Kudi over her online conduct.

Kudi works for Bakare Bukka partly because of her press contacts, and partly because being a Yoruba movie actress doesn't pay well. She is in her mid-fifties and her son and daughter, Tahirah and Khalid, are in their late twenties. That doesn't stop her from getting into Internet fights that embarrass them. She has been temporarily suspended from her personal platforms, and she keeps coming back to make jabs at her opponents and block them.

In one incident, she tweeted that Nollywood actresses should admit how they made their money instead of flexing on Instagram. She was targeting a backstabbing colleague, apparently the mistress of a member of the House of Representatives, who had posted snapshots of her new duplex. A month later, in a lengthy, unpunctuated Facebook post, she went after actresses who contributed to the culture of skin bleaching in Nollywood. That went viral and sparked a national debate. But her most epic retaliation was a YouTube video titled "We Were Almost Destroyed When Our Father Died," in which she narrated, with full hair and makeup done, and as an instrumental version of "(Where Do I Begin?) Love Story" played in the background, how her uncle tried and failed to take over her father's estate.

Kudi got entangled in threads that carried on for months and Sheri, having had enough of reading them, called Enitan to mediate. "What is wrong with my sister?" she asked. "Why is she always behaving like Donald Trump online? Please speak to her because she's not listening to me." Enitan pointed out, as diplomatically as she could, that Sheri and Kudi were alike when it came to returning insults and Sheri yelled, "She uses bad language! I never use bad language!"

The fact that Sheri called it bad language was proof that she didn't swear in English. But she did in Yoruba. She would add a buruku to an insult in a heartbeat, if pushed. Still, Enitan reluctantly called Kudi, who said, "Sister Sheri needs to stop being so bossy. She treats me like her child. She doesn't even treat my children that way. I'm sorry. I know Alhaja raised her and all that, but she takes the whole ọmọluabi thing too seriously. I don't. If you abuse me or my family online, consider yourself trolled."

Indigene

It was no surprise that Kudi was typecast as a shrew from the beginning of her career, but as she carried on defending herself in Yoruba interspersed with English, Enitan had a hard time staying awake because despite her combative nature, Kudi's normal speaking voice was remarkably soothing.

Enitan anticipates the spat between Bakare Bukka and the feminist group will continue to escalate. The more affronted the Bakares are, the more confrontational they become, and Kudi in particular doesn't mind getting street-gutter low to win. But Sheri assures her that they're focusing on what to do if COVID-19 spreads to Nigeria.

"I'm praying it won't reach us here," she says.

"Egypt has announced the first case in Africa," Enitan says.

"Hah? We're in trouble."

"I hope not."

"I heard that black people can't get it."

"Who said?"

"Kudi read it on a blog. Melanin protects us."

"Melanin can't even protect us fully from the sun."

Sheri scowls. "My sister and fake news. You know what she said to me?"

"What?"

"She said I would only be half protected. I told her that if I started on her, her bone-straight wig would turn to a natural-hair one."

"You people won't kill me," Enitan says.

She can only take so much of the Bakares' histrionics, and to this day can't explain why she and Sheri are friends. Their opinions are drastically different, and they don't have shared interests or mutual friends. They probably would never have met had Sheri not stayed with her family during the long vacation before both started secondary school. All they had in common then was that they were girls of the same age in the same Lagos neighborhood.

Enitan would like to think their friendship transcends what happened in their teens when they sneaked out of home to go to a party at Ikoyi Park. Sheri once said rape wasn't her life, and Enitan couldn't decide if she meant what she said or was just dissociating from the stigma. But Sheri got pregnant as a result of being raped at the party and had a botched abortion that could have killed her. She then had to have a hysterectomy, which deprived her of a chance to become a mother. Enitan went through years of guilt because she witnessed the rape, and instead of insisting they report it, she took Sheri to her house, where Sheri had a bath before going home, as if nothing had happened.

Sheri does have ọmọluabi qualities that would make Alhaja proud, but she hasn't always. She was with a sugar daddy when her family were going through the legal dispute with their uncle over their father's estate. She'd recently graduated from university and President Babangida's Structural Adjustment Program was in place. The naira, which had previously been stronger than the dollar, dropped to fifty cents in the foreign exchange market. As it continued to fall, so did values. Sugary girls were notorious back then, but they were loyal to their benefactors and kept low profiles. They can't be compared to runs girls today, who are all over the place now the naira is about three hundred and sixty to the dollar. Runs girls are in lounges and clubs; in Dubai and wherever else they go to shop. They are on Instagram, faces sculpted with makeup, bewigged and flaunting their boob jobs and Brazilian butt lifts. It is no surprise that they run into trouble with cultists, who don't even bother to kidnap them and just lure them in online with the promise of a good life.

On her way to her father's house, Enitan considers how much the landscapes of Ikoyi and Lagos Island at large have changed. If she hadn't witnessed the transformations over the years, she wouldn't be able to find her way around. Ikoyi Park is now Parkview Estate. Banana Island was built on reclaimed land from the lagoon. Part of Lekki is Maroko, which was razed and gentrified. Eko Atlantic is being constructed on land from the ocean, as if Victoria Island is not upscale enough. The state of Lagos might not have a stretch of water left if this pattern continues.

Of the districts on Lagos Island, Ikoyi is the only one that rides on its colonial past, but its status has always been doubtful. After independence, when Lagos was the capital city of Nigeria, Ikoyi did have thriving business, professional and expatriate communities. Its core residents, though, were civil servants who were assigned government homes. They would have been foolish to feel superior while living in accommodation they didn't own. There was also a tacit understanding between out-of-towners like Enitan's father and native Lagosians like Sheri's father that Lagos wasn't no-man's land, no matter what anyone said.

Newer residents are less respectful of this gentleman's agreement over territory and more likely to be smug that they live here, but Ikoyi isn't exactly Mayfair. Parkview Estate, lush with all manner of plant and tree, has its fair share of slumping electricity cables and slanting wooden poles. The buildings clash with one another and the roads are full of potholes.

Enitan drives out of the estate and up Gerard Road with its elevated median and sidewalks, passing imposing blocks of flats where colonial houses once stood. This one Heights. That one Towers. So-and-so Courts. The beautiful homes are conspicuous because they have less competition than they used to, and their electricity generators and water tanks contradict the façade of modernity. She would never buy properties here. They are ridiculously overpriced and can't hedge the exchange rate risk.

She slows down as she approaches Ikoyi Crescent, where her father's house appears diminutive among newer mansions he calls monstrosities. A butterfly flutters across her windshield, startling her. She can't remember the last time she saw one. She does remember riding her bicycle in these parts with her gang of neighbors. They were the Crescent kids, and there were several others—the Queen's Drive kids, the Thompson Avenue kids, the Bourdillon, Cooper and Glover kids. The roads were named after British administrators she knew nothing about. Some were later renamed after Nigerians, Queen's Drive after Lady Oyinkan Abayomi.

In those days, children roamed knowing they weren't completely safe outdoors. They, too, were warned about kidnappers who would use their body parts for juju rituals. They watched news reports on armed robbers like Oyenusi and others, who were executed by gun fire on Bar Beach. They had the civil war, which barely affected Lagos, so she repeated the federal government's propaganda for fun: "To keep Nigeria one is a task that must be done." Her greatest fear was that the Soviet Union and the United States would get into a nuclear war and obliterate Nigeria.

Today's Ikoyi kids meet online as their parents lament about how the Internet exposes them to social ills. Gambling and porn are growing concerns. Drug abuse is a perennial one. Dad, in his youth, may have smoked marijuana with his friends. He and Mum would probably have an older relative or family friend who was never quite the same after recovering from his cocaine addiction, yet they believe their children are more vulnerable than they were. Sons and daughters are at risk in equal measure.

Enitan would say it's normal for preceding generations to be wary of the mass media that influences the next. After all, watching too much television was once frowned upon. She is more concerned about the Internet's propagation of rudeness—the trolling, dragging, calling out and clapping back—in addition to its democratization of fame through influencers. Children don't just worship celebrities anymore. They crave similar attention and adulation, which may seem harmless until they end up like Banx. What she finds strange, and inexcusable, is when adults act like juveniles online, flexing their wealth, sliding into DMs, sending nude photos of themselves and inadvertently uploading their sex tapes. These types of behavior are becoming more and more common.

Ikoyi culture has changed, along with its landscape and residents. Cultures throughout Lagos have, so have cultures elsewhere in Nigeria, since her childhood, and she can't say how much the Internet has contributed to this or blame anyone for being unable to keep up. Neither can she.

The latest anxiety parents have about the Internet is over what they call the attack on the family. It doesn't matter if their marriages are in complete shambles as a result of their actions; they worry that their children are being manipulated by what they refer to as an agenda. Enitan understands their fear. The average straight TV compartmentalizes people who are not. Their rules of conduct are so set that if you're a man who loves to cook or a woman who is outspoken, they might question your sexuality. They can't suddenly be expected to accept non-binary genders or open the floodgates of their imaginations to the idea of fluidity. It will take time to comprehend and accept. As Alabi once said to her, "We haven't settled the matter of gay yet, and they want to add transgender to it."

She first heard the term LGBTQ+ from Yimika and she was curious. Weren't lesbians gay? she asked. Wasn't it offensive to refer to people as queer? Yimika, who had friends of all identities and was versed in the related politics, stubbornly said she didn't know, but Enitan persisted. She had been oblivious, for the most part. Of course she'd heard rumors from her early teens about girls or boys, and later about married men or single men of a certain age. Lesbians could perhaps get away with claiming that no one had asked them out or proposed to them. But she was too busy recovering from heterosexual relationships to pay attention to same-sex ones.

Her father, bless him, told her about two Englishmen who had lived in his house before he bought it as though they were just co-tenants, and she believed him. He often referred to her Uncle Adele, who lived in their hometown and died in his mid-seventies, as a confirmed bachelor. When she was married to Niyi, she sometimes had lunch with his cousin, Jide, an architect. Funny and eloquent, Jide once called Niyi and his brothers a buffoonery of orangutans. They'd bullied him throughout his youth. She had memories of them punching him to make him manlier, and of Niyi's youngest brother advising him that men could turn gay if they didn't find the confidence to chat up women.

Jide lived in a house in Lekki Phase Two with his dogs. He occasionally talked about traveling overseas with someone and only used the pronoun "we." Enitan never asked who he went with. It wasn't her business to. She didn't know any openly gay couples in Nigeria. Why would she? Statutory law criminalized homosexuality, and President Jonathan's Same-Sex Marriage (Prohibition) Bill reinforced the code, once passed. The former was the handiwork of the Church of England, and the latter had Pentecostal written all over it. She found the Jonathan law excessive and its punishment cruel and unusual. She thought parents had good reason to be homophobic from then on, given the risk of their children facing fourteen years in prison, but they weren't as scared of the law as they were of the possibility that their children could be one of the letters.

She didn't pay attention to transgender people either, until they were at the forefront of worldwide panic over the future of civilization. She then had the cis woman exchange with Yimika, who wasn't helpful, so she read a few articles online. Apart from being startled by the number of medical interventions that trans people went through, from prepubescence to adulthood, and by their excessively high murder rates, and wondering about the usual implications for sports and education curricula, she had further questions. Why weren't trans men as vocal as trans women about their issues? How did trans men feel about going to male prisons and using male bathrooms, for instance? Why were feminists at loggerheads with trans women? If the feminists' contention was that women were treated like second-class citizens, wouldn't welcoming trans women to the fold be a way to open their eyes?

She knew her questions would irritate Yimika, so instead she told her an unbelievable story, which happened to be true. She may have had a trans classmate in secondary school. This was in the mid-seventies in Lagos, and she wasn't absolutely sure of the details. It could have been a case of body dysmorphia. Regardless, the girl involved was the only daughter in her family and had several brothers. She was bow-legged and swaggered from side to side, but a lot of other girls in school had distinct walks. She also had a low-cut, as did cool girls when the hairstyle was in fashion.

This girl went to boarding school in England the year Enitan did, and the next thing Enitan heard about her was that she'd died. A mutual classmate said she'd wanted a sex change and choked on a capsule while swallowing it with hot tea. The sex change part baffled Enitan. How was it related to swallowing the capsule? She was too nervous to ask, but the girl's so-called accidental death haunted her for years.

Yimika looked at her in astonishment when she finished the story. "Wow, Mum," she said. "You guys must have been really naive." Enitan said no, TVs weren't a naive generation and neither were Radios. They saw what they wanted to, heard what they wanted to and believed what they wanted to, as Internets did.

Her father is in his favorite chair on the veranda and Auntie Simi, who is back from Atlanta, is with him. He wears a black brocade tunic and trousers, and Auntie Simi a maroon patterned ankara up-and-down and head tie. They are drinking wine and listening to Ebenezer Obey. It is unusually breezy outdoors and Enitan, who has noticed how the weather has turned cooler over the years, wonders if this has anything to do with global warming, but quickly abandons the thought as she joins them.

In the past, she was careful not to get to know her father's—she can't think of a more appropriate term—companions. She was reluctant to do so, even when they made an effort, as it felt like a betrayal of her mother. After her mother died, the feeling intensified and didn't abate until she started dating after her divorce. Only then did she understand her father's position, though she was far more careful than he was. She didn't bring any of her dates home when Yimika was around. She didn't introduce Ladi to Yimika for a good year either and left it up to her to decide how to address him. He was Doctor Akinsanya for a while before he became Uncle Ladi.

Enitan quickly took to Auntie Simi, who often played the role of peacemaker. Whenever Auntie Simi was around, Enitan could count on her to defuse any tensions she had with her father. The last one was over his will. He announced, in Auntie Simi's presence, that he wanted to discuss his will with Enitan and Debayo at a suitable time. Enitan said she never wanted to discuss his will with him. He asked why not, and she said because she'd rather not be reminded of his mortality. He went on about how she ought to be detached and objective about the matter because she was a lawyer. Auntie finally interrupted and said that even Debayo, who carried out autopsies for a living, would be reluctant to discuss his will with him.

Always inclined to make light of bad situations, Auntie Simi relates how her bank debited her current account for text alert charges while she was in Atlanta and her phone was switched off, and refused to reverse them until she threatened to take her money elsewhere.

"It was only forty-eight naira in total," she says, lifting her chin, "but I'd had enough. A bank that can't even guarantee their cards or tokens function. All they ever do is debit accounts for charges. If I sneezed when I walked in, they would have debited my account for it and called it a maintenance charge."

Enitan admires Auntie Simi's ability to seek redress for a customer complaint without getting upset. She hasn't mastered that yet. She is with the same bank, and every time she goes to her local branch, makes a scene because they hoard their thousand-naira notes, claiming they only have five-hundred-naira notes left. Notes that are so filthy they probably have more germs on them than used toilet paper. Yet every year without fail the bank sponsors corporate social responsibility events.

"The worst part is that it's no different from other banks," Auntie Simi says.

"No different at all," Enitan's father says.

"There's no point transferring my money elsewhere."

"No point whatsoever."

"We should start calling it the looting system. Not one of them is in the business of banking."

"Not one."

Enitan pays attention as her father carries on echoing Auntie Simi. He is not usually this quiet when they're together. She keeps an eye on him for early signs of dementia, though he hasn't shown any. He is in the habit of asking, "What happened?" whenever they get cut off during a phone call, as if he can't remember how bad the networks are, but he's done that for years. He doesn't go out much either, but this has been the case since his release from detention. He began to turn down invitations, rather than give people a chance to avoid or pity him at social functions. She has friends who don't know what to do about their surviving parent's loneliness, so is glad that Auntie Simi is back in Lagos. She can leave him for a while knowing he will be fine.

Indigene

Yimika is checking messages on her phone when Enitan gets home in the evening. She lies on the sectional sofa in the sitting room in black leggings and an oversized T-shirt, her braids in a loose bun. On the floor are a can of Schweppes Zobo and a bowl of puff puff. Enitan avoids the offending area and sits in a chair. She would like to ask how Yimika intends to clean up the environment if she can't keep her immediate surroundings tidy. Instead she tells her about the falling-out between Bakare Bukka and the feminist group and asks Yimika to look it up because she doesn't have a Twitter account, or the energy to search for an online row.

Yimika has more time on her hands now that Home Pro has launched and is intrigued enough to assist. She frowns as she scrolls through the tweets. "This is bad."

"Really?"

"Why was Auntie Kudi so triggered?"

"They were as well."

"Yes, but everyone was chill before she and Uncle Gani got involved."

"They're Bakares," Enitan says. "They stick up for each other."

Yimika spent a lot of time with the Bakares when she was younger. They had plenty of children for her to play with. She considers Tahirah and Khalid her cousins, on a par with Ayo and Ola.

"I can't even understand half of what Auntie Kudi is tweeting," she says.

"She was probably typing too fast," Enitan says.

Yimika chuckles. "She could have used spellcheck!"

"What about the group?" Enitan asks. "Look them up."

"Why?"

"I want to know who they are."

"Mum, don't start. No one cares which families they're from."

"Go on," Enitan pleads.

She researches people's backgrounds in the course of work and inherited her interest from her mother, who had enough information on Lagos society to qualify as a genealogist. She already has a profile of the founders of the feminist group in mind. They will be in their late twenties to early thirties. They would probably have had some education overseas. Their families would most likely be of means.

She is right. Yimika finds their website and learns that the father of one of the founders is the CEO of an oil company, and the other's is a government minister. She's heard enough about the two men to deduce that they make their families miserable with side-chick romps. The sort of men who would be quite happy to have their wives nurse their sorrows in churches, so long as their wives don't end up sleeping with pastors, they would be delighted that their daughters are feminists. They might even encourage their daughters to be radical ones, hoping they won't be sluts if they hate men enough.

"You see?" Enitan says.

She appreciates moments like this, when she can show Yimika her instincts aren't always off.

"No, I don't," Yimika says. "What have their fathers got to do with anything?"

Enitan hesitates. She has to be cautious. Yimika has never actually called herself a feminist, but she uses terms like toxic masculinity, mansplaining and slut-shaming.

"They're daughters of patriarchy," Enitan says.

"Meaning?"

"They benefit from it."

Yimika eyes her. "With all the sexism that goes on here?"

Enitan tucks her chin in. "What sexism have you faced in Nigeria?"

"Mum, I don't have to spell it out."

"No, seriously. I'd like to know. I've told you some of mine."

Most recently, she told Yimika about her limited Me Too experiences in Lagos—a bank colleague who would catcall her in the office, a client of Taiwo and Associates who constantly made suggestive remarks and a friend of her father's who once groped her bottom while hugging her at Ikoyi Club, and did it so swiftly she thought she was mistaken. She said Nigeria couldn't have a Me Too movement because it would be the undoing of men and boys in every family, from grandfather to grandson.

Yimika raises her hand and voice. "We're in a country where men can marry multiple women and get away with marrying girls."

"You, in particular, I mean."

"I don't have to say more than that. The level of sexism here is problematic."

Problematic—yet another word that Enitan picked up from Yimika.

"Sexism can be problematic for men as well," she says.

"In what way?"

"If they're expected to pay for everything."

"Boo hoo."

"I'm just trying to be impartial."

Yimika frowns. "You can't be impartial about a situation that's blatantly unfair. How can women benefit from patriarchy, anyway?"

Enitan again hesitates. She's accustomed to proving she is right and sounding authoritative even when she isn't. Yimika is more likely to badger her and put her on the defensive.

"Through wealth and status," she says, "from our fathers and husbands."

"That doesn't mean we can't be victims of it."

"You're right. We are. In cases of rape and domestic violence—"

"And sexual assault. And sexual harassment."

"Yes, overwhelmingly more than men, but being a victim doesn't necessarily absolve us of liability."

"Mum, please stop trying to play devil's advocate. It's annoying and it's giving pick me vibes."

"Hear what I'm saying. People don't challenge systems that benefit them on the whole."

"You haven't even been to their website to read their mission statement!"

"I don't have to."

"Why not?"

"Because the founders aren't being honest, Yimz. They're hurt and angry and have every right to be, but being hurt and angry isn't enough to make a movement. What have they done for women and girls, for a start?"

"Mum, I have friends who have trouble finding flats to rent because they're single women. At least they're talking about issues like that."

"Please. Anyone can talk and your friends can easily get their parents to back them. Women in this country barely earn enough to cover their rent. I'm sorry, but we can't keep going on about inequalities between Naija men and women if we won't address inequalities between Naija women."

"That's a different issue."

"No, it's not. Our biggest divide isn't between men and women. It's between people who have financial freedom and everyone else."

"It's still not the same issue and we can't do anything about it."

"We can. We just don't care enough to, and until someone does, the group can have their say, but they should forget about having a movement because it won't get far."

Enitan has never taken time to read feminist theory and doesn't know if it addresses the peculiar position of Nigerian women like the founders of the group, but she knows their story well because it is hers. They are raised to believe they can achieve whatever they want to by studying hard. They outperform boys in schools and colleges, here and abroad. They continue to be competitive in their careers until their late twenties, when they are told, if they haven't already learned, that they will have to diminish themselves to get married. They don't want to be equal to men in general; they specifically want to have the same rights as men in their social circles, which is fine. But they're not just better off than most Nigerian men, they're better off than most Nigerian women. So if they truly cared about equality for women, they should be willing to give up some of the advantages they enjoy to women who don't. She doubts their mission statement has such a provision and anything short of that can only inspire a trend.

"Your views are too rigid," Yimika says.

"Of course they are, and feminism should be more than getting into Twitter rows."

"That's not all they do, and you're taking this one a little too personally."

"Of course I am."

Enitan never told Yimika about what happened to Sheri because it would be a breach of trust, but Kudi must have been ten or eleven and she would have known. She would also have known that Sheri fought off her sugar daddy, when he physically assaulted her, and then left him.

Kudi herself married a man from a polygamous Lagos Muslim family. He sold imported cars and was doing well—enough to order her to give up her career because he felt it was unbecoming for a married woman to be an actress. Kudi didn't even argue with him. She left with Tahirah and Khalid and moved in with her mother. That was when her backstabbing colleague went around saying that she was homeless. Their families had mediation after mediation. Self-proclaimed online in-laws, who adjudicated public marital breakups, gave their opinions, but no one could persuade Kudi to go back to her husband.

"Mark my words," Enitan adds. "If the founders ever get married, as I'm sure they will with enough family pressure, they'll put up with more than Auntie Sheri and Auntie Kudi ever did. Internalized sexism, my arse."

Yimika sighs. "Okay, Mum. You've made your point."

Enitan isn't sure she has, but venting has been satisfying.

She wants Yimika to question what she hears, even from her. She remembers having to get written consent from Niyi to apply for a new passport when she was married to him and thinking, This can't be possible in 1996. Not until 2009 was the requirement dropped, following a landmark lawsuit: *Dr. Priye Iyalla-Amadi v. Nigerian Immigration Services*. She researched the case and the parties involved and discovered that the plaintiff, a college professor, was married to the writer Elechi Amadi, and her lawyer, Busola Olagunju, was Brigadier Benjamin Adekunle's daughter. She can recall other instances when she could have successfully challenged the law and did nothing but talk. What would she look like telling her daughter that she's a victim of sexism?

"Am I forgiven?" she asks.

"Yes," Yimika snaps.

From then on, Enitan takes note of circumstances relating to their exchange, when she has reason to. She was playing devil's advocate, but she wants to be sure she wasn't dismissing Yimika's opinions while trying to justify hers.

Monday morning, she has a meeting with Dagogo and Alabi, and they discuss, among other matters, who to delegate the task of supervising junior associates to during their legal writing courses. They have a choice between Muyiwa and Fisayo, another senior associate, and they all agree that Fisayo is the right person for the job.

"Muyiwa is too calm," Alabi says. "We need someone who will make sure they show up on time and stop them from leaving early. You know how juniors can be if you give them a chance."

"One excuse after another," Dagogo says.

"Fisayo won't stand for that," Enitan says.

Dagogo nods. "She's tough."

"Like her mother," Alabi says.

Fisayo's mother, a Lagos state judge, has a reputation for being exacting. She will embarrass any lawyer who comes to court unprepared. Dagogo and Alabi are wary of her. Enitan finds her reasonably agreeable, but is friendly enough with Fisayo to know that mother and daughter have been at odds on the subject of marriage. Fisayo is fed up with her mother pressuring her to "find someone to settle down with."

Wednesday afternoon, Enitan gets around to meeting with Fisayo about the training courses. At work, Fisayo wears heels that make her appear taller and pulls her hair back in a ponytail. Enitan wouldn't describe her as tough, but she might say Fisayo has a direct manner that can intimidate juniors and offend clients who expect lawyers to show deference.

Enitan asks after her mother and Fisayo says, "We're not speaking to each other right now."

"Why not?" Enitan asks.

"She won't stop harassing me about marriage," Fisayo says. "Is marriage by force?"

Enitan says yes, marriage is indeed by force. She wouldn't want to cross the judge, and she, too, would like Yimika to get married in a few years and have children. Would she pressure her daughter? No, but she might drop a hint or two and pray for her on the quiet.

Friday evening, she has dinner with Ladi at an Italian restaurant on Victoria Island that offers a service as fine as dining gets in Lagos. A young couple seated at a table nearby get her attention. They are in their mid-twenties and not the usual guests. The woman wears a long wavy wig with a side parting and the man a polo shirt with his collar up. They ignore their cocktails and scroll through their iPhones as they wait for their meals. They could easily fit the profiles of a Yahoo boy and runs girl, but they look too wholesome. He is probably a bank worker or an Uber driver and she is probably a girlfriend he's doing his best to impress.

Yimika is somewhere else on Victoria Island having drinks with her friends. Enitan can just hear them referring to guys

Indigene

they know as niggas and fuck boys, and talking about the streets of Lagos being tough, as if dating is a criminal activity. Their mimicry of hip-hop culture as revealing as their clothes, they may not need anyone to buy them iPhones or take them to expensive restaurants, but it makes her nervous that it's normal for them to meet partners on apps and have hookups.

She tells Ladi that she feels guilty about going out with him when Yimika isn't dating, but he doesn't encourage her.

"She's having a good time," he says. "So should you."

It's all right for him to say, she thinks. He doesn't have ovaries and his children are married.

She's heard that women in villages reach menopause and simply retire their reproductive organs. They retreat to their huts, leaving their husbands to younger wives, and turn their attention to looking after their grandchildren. She thinks there's dignity in doing that. She and her peers keep trying to get attention from men, preventing wrinkles with serums and creams, tucking their gray hair under wigs and squeezing themselves into body-shaping underwear. Making every effort to prolong their sex lives.

Saturday morning, an old girl in her secondary school WhatsApp group turns sixty, and the group status is updated with her photo, which looks as if it was taken at a wedding. The OG wears a tight-fitting lace gown and fan-style gele. A caption underneath says, "Our Birthday Girl!" The administrator posts a message of felicitations that ends with profuse prayers and various emojis—hearts, balloons, confetti and champagne. Other OGs post similar messages. Enitan reads them before typing hers. She is light on prayer and doesn't use emojis.

They attended the best secondary school for girls in Nigeria, which admitted top Common Entrance candidates from every state, most of whom were boarders. Their school was federally funded, so its fees were nominal and students whose families couldn't afford them received scholarships. Colonial to the core when it was founded, it gained independence under its first Nigerian principal and was a sanctuary of unity during the civil war. Enitan was part of the class that started after the war, and she and her schoolmates had a camaraderie that endured, despite their different backgrounds. They were a select number of girls who were given a head start, and they became lawyers, doctors, bankers, business owners and so on.

Now they're in the final quartile of their careers at home and abroad. They are single, married, divorced or widowed. Most of them are mothers and a few are already grandmothers. Apart from birthday greetings on their forum, they post invitations to social functions and information about fundraising projects because their school, like most public educational institutions, is rundown. Occasionally, they also post photos of events they attend, rare black-and-white shots from their school days, inspirational messages and funny skits. Posts about politics aren't encouraged, though, because politics remains polarized along ethnic and religious lines. If an OG so much as criticizes the current administration, another OG will tell her not to speak bad over Nigeria, as opposed to speaking life into her hopes for Nigeria. Praying for Nigeria is always apropos. Prayer in general is.

Enitan isn't a churchgoer. She prays in bed, in the shower or in her car and enjoys certain hymns. That's about it. But there was a time she couldn't have a casual conversation with other women in Lagos without getting preached to, and in born-again lingo that put her off—led by the spirit, anointed by God, walking in faith. Kini kan, kini kan. This one, that one.

Indigene

She once had a conversation with a woman who believed the story of Adam and Eve. The woman was a psychiatrist, so Enitan brought up Darwin and the Big Bang theory, assuming the woman would recognize her cognitive dissonance. Instead, the woman said Enitan was too rational and didn't have to make sense of the word of God. She had to come to Jesus like a little child; otherwise, she would never enter the kingdom of heaven. All that while shutting her eyes and raising a hand.

This was at the height of Pentecostalism in Lagos, and the women in question were raised as either Catholics or Protestants. One or two were Muslims who had converted to Christianity, and they are just as fervent. These days, she finds all of them less intrusive. Perhaps their churches are packed full and their pastors no longer require them to evangelize, or perhaps they've become jaded while waiting for blessings. Before, they would end conversations with "God bless," then that changed to "Stay blessed." Now it's just "Bless," as if God is no longer material.

The next Friday, Enitan has dinner with Ladi at his house. Mama Titi cooked a stew she can't resist. It has bitesize pieces of beef, bọkọtọ and ṣaki and is simmered to perfection. Enitan has learned to stay out of the kitchen when Mama Titi is there. She suspects that Mama Titi, apart from being territorial, is disappointed that she isn't woman enough to fight for control. After Mama Titi leaves, she boils rice and fries dodo to go with the stew, adding three rings of fresh onion to the rice, as her mother used to, and cutting the plantains into cubes, as Ladi prefers.

He's been having a hard time getting his staff to observe his new safety protocols and is unusually moody. At times like this, she will cook, even if he thinks it's funny to react by pretending he's having a heart attack. She favors his kitchen over hers because it is more spacious. The rest of his house is functional at best, with furniture that's sturdy and easy to maintain. In his sitting room, he has an HP printer plonked on top of a wooden wall console and calls it decoration. If she suggests he buy home accents, he asks, each time, "What will they do for me?"

They eat at his dining table as the air conditioner hums and talk about the Federal Ministry of Health's confirmation of the first case of COVID-19 in Nigeria. Earlier in the week, an Italian man flew into Lagos from Milan and spent a night at a hotel before heading to Ogun State, where he presented at a medical center with symptoms and was put in isolation. He has since been transferred to a containment facility in Lagos, and people who have been in contact with him are being traced.

Enitan asks if the health ministry will be able to handle the case.

"They have a system in place," Ladi says.

"Yes, but will it work?"

"That's another matter."

"You have to be careful, love."

"Everyone has to."

She reaches out and rubs his shoulder. She is more dependent on him than she's willing to admit.

Saturday morning at her flat, she interviews a housegirl recommended by an OG. Her name is Happiness, and she shows up in a cropped tawny wig, black T-shirt dress, purple plastic clogs and a faux Louis Vuitton bag.

"Good day, ma," she says, with a smile and curtsy.

"Happiness," Enitan says. "How are you?"

"I'm fine, ma."

"Come, let's sit down and talk."

Indigene

They do so at the dining table, where Happiness looks for an unobtrusive spot on the floor to put her bag. Enitan asks questions about her job and salary. She knows Happiness is twenty-three and has been a housegirl since she dropped out of secondary school. Her current employers are about to emigrate to Canada and Happiness says she's been with them for five years. She lives in their boys' quarters and they pay her monthly. She's had interviews with a few of their friends, but is looking for a job that will allow her to stay on in Lekki.

"Do you have children?" Enitan asks.

"Only one, ma."

"Boy or girl?"

"Boy."

"What's his name?"

Happiness beams. "Excellence."

"Excellence," Enitan says with relish. "How old is he?"

"Six," Happiness says, "but he will reach seven by March."

"You must have had him quite young."

"Yes, ma. I fell pregnant when I was sixteen and put to bed after I reached seventeen."

Enitan knows better than to ask about Excellence's father, but the boys' quarters on her estate aren't big enough to accommodate mother and son, and they were built without cooking facilities.

"Our BQ is small," she says, regretfully.

Happiness sits up. "He's not with me, ma. He's with my mother in the village."

Enitan studies her keen expression. "That can't be easy."

"He's okay, ma. I see him when I go home. Lagos is too hard to work and look after him."

Enitan nods in agreement. She had to leave work early to pick up Yimika from school and took days off to nurse her through illnesses. She was only able to do that because she worked for her father's firm and had a nanny.

"Are you sure you can manage?" she asks.

"Yes, ma," Happiness says. "I will manage as I've been managing."

Enitan offers Happiness a higher salary and Happiness accepts it and thanks her without an excessive show of gratitude. None of that unwarranted "God bless you" business. She will start work in April. She wants to visit her mother and Excellence beforehand. Enitan likes her confidence, but is reluctant to go back to the habitual ways of keeping people in check while relying on them.

She told Bright off over the burnt-sofa incident. She told Julius off as well for driving recklessly, and they both looked as mystified as her artisans. Their usual trick was to irritate her at inconvenient moments by pointing out an electrical gadget was broken or her car needed petrol. She kept her valuables locked up in her bedroom, so as not to encourage Bright to steal. She couldn't even trust Julius to buy petrol without cheating her or using her car as a taxi on his way, but she was lucky. The incidence of disgruntled staff killing their employers is on the rise. Dagogo has come up with terms for this—ogacide and madamcide.

Later that afternoon, Enitan decides to replace a fluorescent bulb in her kitchen that has been flickering all week, to her annoyance. She heads out to Prince Ebeano Supermarket on Admiralty Way, one of the few places on Lagos Island that sell incandescent fluorescent bulbs. Everywhere else has LED bulbs, which are more in demand. This is an errand Yimika could run, but she is visiting her grandfather and it shouldn't take Enitan more than thirty minutes.

As she steps out of her building into the front yard, which is paved with interlocking bricks, two uniformed daytime gatemen greet her and bow. Sometimes they startle her while she's busy searching for her car keys or her mind is elsewhere. They work on rotation with nighttime gatemen and are always on the alert, not so much for armed robbers as for tenants who might give them money. She returns their waves as she drives out of the premises in her Highlander.

She gets to Ebeano's, which sells every import from hair extensions to toilet plungers, and the bulbs she is looking for are out of stock. An assistant suggests she go to their Chevron branch to see if they have any. That branch is in Lekki Phase Two. She expects she can make it there in forty minutes, if the traffic is in her favor. She often drove to Lekki Two when she was buying paintings for her flat, but she no longer goes to the arts and crafts market there. Some of her paintings were mounted on untreated boards that got infested with wood borers, and she later had to have the boards replaced.

There is a bottleneck on her side of the expressway, which begins at the first roundabout she joins and continues as far as she can see. Two extra lanes have formed parallel to the usual three, and drivers maneuver in and out of all five, honking their horns and revving their engines. Enitan, with her car air conditioner on, listens to a radio station that plays old-school music as she ignores traders who weave between vehicles. Some stand by her window displaying their wares, one with several wheel covers around his neck. She is forced to shake her head repeatedly. No, she doesn't want a bottle of groundnuts. No, she doesn't want an imported self-help book that's probably pirated, and no, she definitely doesn't want to buy free water from a questionable source.

Behind them is the backdrop of Lekki. Not the businesses on the main roads of commercial Phase One. Nor the warehouses, car dealerships, events centers and megachurches of industrial Phase Two. Not even the ubiquitous billboards that advertise every product and service from alcohol to redemption. But pedestrians and commuters who don't own cars, hundreds of them, hurrying along, running across the expressway or standing around waiting for public and commercial transport to and from the island. They go by Bus Rapid Transit coaches, danfo minibuses, korope microbuses, by ride-share cars, okada motorcycles and kẹkẹ tricycles, all of which vie for space with lorries, trucks and tankers.

Enitan anticipates that any time soon, an official in a Toyota Prado will try and cut through the traffic, with a Toyota Tacoma in front sounding a siren and one or two behind occupied by armed policemen, but this doesn't happen. She avoids making eye contact with the beggars who approach her window. A woman goes from car to car holding twin babies in her arms. A paraplegic man rolls his wheelchair backwards as he pleads for alms. They are displaced northerners who have fled areas of religious violence, but she has read newspaper articles that claim they are managed by syndicates and that the mothers would rather beg than work and use each other's babies as props.

She has come to accept that there is no point giving child beggars money. If she does, more will come, and they are unnervingly practiced at praying with trembling voices and paying false compliments. They don't give up easily on gambling that every indifferent expression hides a conscience, and offer on-the-spot cleaning services if necessary. A girl in a faded brown dress and pink turban begins to wipe Enitan's windshield with a cloth. She has a bottle of soapy water tucked under her other arm. Enitan shoos her away. Unfazed, the girl walks on. She doesn't appear underfed, but her growth has definitely been stunted. The traffic moves and Enitan drives forward quickly to prevent cars on either side of hers from switching lanes.

She continues this way, as if she is in a slow-motion obstacle race, passing the exit to Nike Art Gallery and the one to Lekki arts and crafts market and approaches yet another crossroads. The sign to Osapa London amuses her, as does a street clown in a shower cap and white sunglasses who dances between vehicles. She stays in the far-right lane that leads to Chevron. There are more traders and beggars here. At a bus stop to her left, a group of young men, who look like ọmọ onilẹ, gather around their ringleader, whose hair is bleached blond. Even at a distance they appear to be high on drugs. On the grassy elevated median, a northern girl in a dingy orange dress and blue turban hugs the base of a streetlight as a boy in an ankara shirt and shorts, who may be her brother, does a dangerous cartwheel. Enitan looks beyond them to ShopRite Circle Mall, which was practically burned down last year and has since been closed to the public. Going by news reports, the perpetrators were either protesting the killings of Nigerians in South Africa or using the killings as an excuse to loot. She was sure most of them were ọmọ onilẹ, who are more active in Lekki Two. The money they extort from people who buy land and property in their territory can never be enough.

The traffic light changes to red as she reaches the top of the lane. In an opposing lane, the driver of a battered korope crammed with passengers runs the light and gets stuck in the middle of the crossroads. A yellow-and-maroon-checked Lagos State Traffic Management Authority car is stationed ahead, and an officer, who stands next to it in a uniform of the same colors, raises his hand at the korope driver.

No one wants to get in trouble with LASTMA. No amount of begging will help. Enitan has seen drivers abandon their vehicles on the roads altogether, patapata, for impoundment, rather than pay a fine. She watches this korope driver do the daftest left turn ever to escape the officer, swerving past vehicles in the lane across hers until he misjudges a space and bumps the front corner of her car.

"Shit," she whispers.

The driver comes to a stop. Within a second there is gridlock at the crossroads. The honking and revving increases as onlookers watch. Enitan gets out of her car with her heart racing and shuts her door while the driver stays in his korope and holds his head.

"Are you mad?" she yells at him.

He drops his head to his steering wheel as the officer marches towards them.

"You'll see," Enitan says, snapping her fingers. "LASTMA has caught you today. Very good."

Already sweaty, she inspects the damage. His korope barely dented her car but has left a stain of white paint on it. She reaches out to touch it, and a stocky man in jeans and an oil-smudged T-shirt with a caption that reads "Choose life" appears at her side. Before she can protest, he crouches and begins to clean the stain with a damp rag.

"What are you doing?" she yells.

"I de rub karosin!"

She gesticulates. "Why are you rubbing kerosene on my car, for God's sake?"

"I wan clean am for you!"

"Who asked you to?"

"Don't worry, ma!"

"Stop! You'll damage the paint!"

"It can't damage! I mix it with water!"

Enitan momentarily shuts her eyes in despair—the commotion, the sun, the man. He must be a roadside mechanic as well as a crash entrepreneur. She can't decide if ordinary circumstances are extraordinary in Lagos, or extraordinary circumstances are ordinary.

He finishes his task within seconds and stands up heroically. "Look am!"

Enitan takes a deep breath expecting to find further damage. The stain has disappeared and she is relieved, but she shakes her head. "I'm not giving you any money."

He grins. "Mummy..."

"No. I'm not your mother and you can't hustle me."

"I'm not ozzling!"

"Say whatever you want. I'm not going to pay you."

He walks off looking aggrieved and she strides back to her car. Inside, she composes herself and watches the korope driver prostrate himself before the LASTMA officer. She is right on both counts about ordinary and extraordinary circumstances.

Forty-five minutes later, she arrives at the Chevron branch of Ebeano's. She tells herself she needs a driver. A driver would have saved her the trouble today. She finds the bulbs she is looking for, packaged in long narrow boxes, takes two of them and puts them in her cart.

She is second in line at a cash register. The woman ahead of her, twentysomething with a black head wrap, has a shopping cart of various items and loads them onto the counter. The cashier, also a woman, rings them up. Enitan gives them adequate space. She has stood in lines where customers press against each other for no apparent reason.

She is still in the same spot when a man in his thirties, with sunglasses perched on his head, walks over and slips into the space before her. He holds a pack of toothpaste and tub of hair oil.

"Excuse me," Enitan says, from behind. "There's a queue, you know."

The man turns around, his eyes a little too red. "I was here before."

"So?" Enitan asks.

"I went to get hair oil."

"And?" His head is shaved bald. What does he need hair oil for?

He faces the woman, who has finished loading her drinks onto the counter. "Wasn't I here before?"

"You were," the woman answers in a nasal voice.

"He could still have joined the line," Enitan says, glaring at the woman, then at the cashier, who appears to have perked up at the prospect of a dispute.

The woman turns her face away as if Enitan is yet another big madam she can't contend with. She retrieves her wallet and pays the cashier as the man squares his shoulders and stays put.

Enitan is incapable of reasoning at times like this. She got into an argument with a trader at Lekki arts and crafts market while they were bargaining. He told her to go to Nike Art Gallery if she wasn't prepared to pay his final price for a painting. Better people, he said, would buy it. She walked out of his store and hasn't been back. She got into another argument in an electronics shop on Victoria Island. The cashier was about to attend to an Indian man who cut ahead of the line she was in. She told the cashier she would leave the fans she was about to buy and would never ever, lai lai, shop there again. She is a Karen when it comes to shopping, but she can just hear Yimika reminding her to check her privilege and Ladi warning her to be careful, so she says nothing else.

Sunday March the 8th is International Women's Day, on which banks and other commercial businesses hold token summits on women's issues and newspapers publish lists of powerful women that weak women should emulate. Yimika is asleep in her bedroom when Enitan sits at the dining table and glances through one of them over her breakfast of akara and pineapple juice. It has the usual crew—the richest woman in the country, a former finance minister, a bank CEO, a television and film producer, and a megachurch pastor-cum-motivational speaker.

To Enitan, lists like this might as well be titled "Nyah-nyah-nyah Nyah-nyah." They smack of an outdated girl-boss feminism that Yimika derides. Further down are nominees who probably paid or lobbied to be recognized. There's a woman who is praised for her charity work, even as her banker husband is being charged by the Economic and Financial Crimes Commission with embezzlement. There is a "Queen of Interior Design," which suggests Her Royal Highness's ego is out of control to approve of such a title. After her is a woman who is described as iconic. Her skin is so lightened she looks like an advert for glutathione intravenous therapy. Isioma's face pops up next, in a heavily edited glamor shot, followed by a self-commendation about putting prison reform on the map.

Copycat, dirty rat, Enitan thinks.

Instances like this do take her back, not quite to being a two-year-old, but a young girl in a playground. She'd be swinging on her own and someone would sit in the next swing and start going faster and faster to get higher than her, hoping she might compete. Even then she knew the best thing to do was to continue at her own pace. She is no closer to reaching a decision about Indigene and will not be rushed. She considers it a blessing not to have the impulse that ladies who launch and their groupies have. They can't see an activity that might put them in the spotlight without wanting to crash it and claim it as theirs.

She turns the page and reads a somewhat unctuous column about the prospect of Nigeria electing a female president, written by a man who says women need more representation in government and should be given opportunities to run for office. He is a sitting senator, so perhaps he's distancing himself from the National Assembly's failure to pass gender equality bills. This is precisely what Enitan was trying to tell Yimika about. The repetition of ideas without questioning their viability in Nigeria, whether it pertains to who espouses them and why, who gets ahead and how, or who is exploited and subdued by whom. Which women are most likely to run for president? How will they win elections and what will they do afterward? Because if they have the same mindset as men who use chicanery to get political positions, they certainly won't represent her. And if they are charged with crimes while they're in office, they can say all they want about sexism and double standards in the government, they won't have her sympathy.

She doesn't mention the column to Yimika, who finally gets out of bed midmorning in a rumpled green T-shirt with a caption that says "I like shenanigans." They don't have to share the same opinions, despite the evidence she's gathered to support hers. She gives Yimika time to settle into her breakfast of pounded yam and ẹgusi before asking what time she came home last night.

"Um," Yimika mumbles. "About three."

"You're slipping," Enitan says.

"Sorry," Yimika says. "The party didn't start until midnight."

"You have to be careful."

"I know, I know. Cultists."

Enitan isn't absolutely sure the stories about cultists using young women for rituals are true. Ladi thinks it's more likely that illegal organ harvesting is on the rise.

"It's not a joke, Yimz," she insists. "I didn't make up the stories."

Yimika is condescendingly calm. "I hear you, but my friends stay out late, too, and Dad says Lagos is safer than it's been for a while."

Enitan knows this tactic and it doesn't faze her. "He lives on Banana Island. The only people he needs protection from are social climbers."

Yimika bobs her shoulders in amusement. For all her affinity with her father, she won't live with him. She wouldn't try half of what she does at home with his wife around.

Her expression turns serious. "Mum, is it me or are there more sex workers on Admiralty Way?"

"It's not you," Enitan says. "Why?"

"I saw so many of them on my way home and I was like . . ." Yimika narrows her eyes.

Enitan sees them as well, in the evenings and at night. She called them prostitutes until Yimika told her that was a pejorative term. She thinks this is no different from calling a prison a correctional center.

"It's hardship, my dear," she says. "I see more of them in Kirikiri as well."

"Sad," Yimika murmurs.

The following week at her office, Enitan gets a call from Busola Aderemi, a family friend and former neighbor at Sunrise Estate.

"Hallo, Eni?"

Busola will shorten a name like no other and her voice is like a baritone horn.

"Hey," Enitan says. "This is a surprise. How are you?"

"Very well, thanks. I've just come back from a short trip to Old Blighty."

Only Busola would call England Old Blighty in jest. She is also in a permanent state of leaving or returning to Nigeria and will offer this information unsolicited.

"How are things there?" Enitan asks, referring to COVID-19.

"Ugh," Busola says. "London has completely lost its character."

"Hm."

"Remember how it was when we were in school? London was London then. Now it's full of immigrants. Full of them—Albanians, Poles and people of color or whatever they're called—and they're so rude. English people are usually polite when you get to see them, yet they're constantly being told they owe immigrants an apology."

Busola is against what she calls wokery. She would never accept a term like people of color applies to her and believes that London is overrun with immigrants she refuses to acknowledge as British. She hates Meghan and Harry—Meghan more than Harry—and said their behavior would never be tolerated in a Nigerian royal family, let alone by the hoi polloi. For her, Megxit and Brexit are timely.

Enitan is indifferent to either departure. Meghan wouldn't be spared in a traditional Yoruba family, that's for sure. She would have to get on both knees to greet her mother-in-law, and every fat-bottomed aunt would lecture her about being too skinny and chastise her if she failed to perform her duties. They might even accuse her of using juju to control her husband and divide their family.

As for Brexit, countries go through shifts of all kinds. This is how it's always been. Britain, in addition, suffers from the identity crisis that territories it once occupied chronically endure, as its cultures are demonized, its history is revised and its monarchy continues to dwindle. What surprises Enitan, if anything, is the rise of British media mercenaries who profiteer from internal conflicts. They are very American.

"In other words, it wasn't a good trip," she says.

"It was, actually," Busola says. "I got some rest and caught up with the kids."

"Aw, that's good."

"Anyway, enough about me. How are you?"

"The same. Nothing new to report."

"Sorry I haven't come over to see you. I know Lekki's only a hop, skip and jump away, but the traffic . . ."

What part of Lagos is a hop, skip and jump away? Enitan thinks, picturing Busola doing all three.

"There's traffic everywhere," she says.

"Yes, but it's getting worse on the island. Just driving from my house to my office wears me out."

Busola lives in Ikoyi and goes to her Victoria Island office on an ad hoc basis. Presumably, she can't cope with crossing Falomo Bridge.

"You drive yourself to work?" Enitan teases her.

"Me? I wouldn't even drive myself next door in this place."

Enitan shakes her head in amazement. Busola, Busola. What will anyone do with her? Still speaking in an English public school accent at the age of fifty-nine, still thinking she's a Sloane in the year 2020, and still deliberately making outrageous statements and pretending she doesn't know why people call her a snob. This is her way. She playacts all the time and has done so for as long as Enitan has known her. Her playacting gets impressionable clients to hire her for PR services and is a tradition of sort on her mother's side of the family.

Busola's mother was from what Enitan's mother would call a good family. Her father was a pre-independence politician, and her mother a Lagos socialite. They both attended college in England. He studied classics and she, domestic science. Busola once showed Enitan a black-and-white photo of her grandmother posing in a tweed cap and matching knickerbockers, complete with shirt, tie and tights. The photo was apparently taken at a studio in Lagos, which made Enitan wonder why Busola's grandmother, who looked way ahead of her time, wasn't perspiring.

Busola's grandparents sent her mother to England at the age

Indigene

of sixteen to complete her education, and she returned to Lagos with a sociology degree and been-to mannerisms—speaking the King's or Queen's English, wearing hats to tea parties and all that. She was meant to marry a man of similar standing, but she ended up with Busola's father, a lawyer, who was an out-of-towner and the only one in his family to get a degree from an English university. After independence, he was made a federal minister in the First Republic and soon acquired an inexplicably ostentatious lifestyle. He bought land and property throughout Lagos, and once he retired from politics, invested in multinationals during the indigenization policy years, when a limited share of their business assets had to be in the hands of Nigerians. He did the same during the privatization and deregulation years in the banking and telecom sectors. He was a chairman and director of several companies.

Busola went to prep school in England at the age of ten, and Enitan, who went to boarding school there at the age of fourteen, had nothing but empathy for her. She could just imagine her in uniform, skin and hair dry, and subjected to God knows what. During half-term breaks, Busola and her elder brother, Kayode, and younger sister, Ronke, stayed at their parents' flat in Chelsea. Their mother was always there, their father rarely so. Busola found out he had another family in Lagos around the time Enitan's parents separated and they bonded over their mutual disillusionment. Enitan spent half-terms with her father at his flat on Baker Street. She would meet Busola at Sloane Square tube station and they would walk King's Road together. Enitan would be bundled up in a coat, and Busola, who was more accustomed to the weather, would wear corduroy jeans, pastel-colored sweaters and pearls.

Enitan never had enough pocket money to shop on King's Road. Oxford Street was her haunt—Miss Selfridge for the latest fashion and Marks and Sparks for underwear. On King's Road, she would browse around and chat with Busola, who felt she was the odd one out in her family. Kayode was her mother's favorite and Ronke was her father's, according to her. She would call her father a total idiot and her mother a stupid cow. Enitan would be fascinated to the point of nervousness by her verbal outbursts. No Nigerian she knew spoke about their parents that way, no matter how oyinbo-ish they were.

They grew apart when Enitan started university in London. Busola committed the ultimate act of rebellion against her parents by telling them she wanted a gap year. She took off to Paris for two years, and when she returned to London, got a job at a PR company. She then began to mix with a clique of Nigerian students known as the High Socs. Enitan, who had grown up with some of them in Lagos, wasn't keen on continuing ties. Her father never spoiled her with money, so she found it embarrassing to be associated with people who were. She had her own crowd in London, who were less insular.

She asks after Busola's husband, Wale, who is a senator.

"He's fine," Busola says. "He's in Abuja."

"What's happening there?"

"As I always say, the lodgers of the boys' quarters have taken over the main house."

Busola considers Wale's colleagues in the House of Assembly unrefined and describes them as local. She is particularly scornful of those who attempt to outdo her by namedropping or boasting about their material possessions. She says they are naff.

Like her mother, she ended up marrying a man outside her social circle when she came back to Nigeria. She met Wale at Lagos Polo Club. No one knew what he did for a living, but he wore good suits and drove nice cars. He was a prince, and as such was given much respect in his hometown, but women like Busola had intricate rules for assessing their prospective husbands. Being royalty wasn't a big deal. There were many of them around. Having a common ethnic background wasn't a major concern, either. That was for tribalistic plebs to worry about. Having a university degree was a must, even though Busola herself didn't have one yet. Wale got his from Holborn Law Tutors in London, after which he attended law school in Lagos. Speaking English well helped him, and speaking Yoruba showed he had a sense of national pride. However, Nigerian and foreign pronunciations couldn't cross-contaminate, so Wale's fluency in Yoruba was okay, as long as he didn't drop or add Hs to English words.

For Busola, a man who had made a name for himself wasn't quite enough, even if his name was a household one. His family's reputation had to be pre-established and the farther back it dated the better, more so if he stood to inherit property. He couldn't go around asking, "Do you know who I am?" because that would be a sure sign he didn't belong in her circle. They had their ways of letting people know who was who. Busola's tactic was to intimidate upstarts with minutiae about her travels around Europe. For example, the fact that she'd eaten the best spaghetti carbonara in a village restaurant near Lugano. Showing off about wealth was a no-no to her, but it didn't matter how wealth was acquired. Everyone in her circle was related to someone who wasn't above-board. Wale's money apparently came from a bank loan he defaulted on.

Wale was snobbish in his own way. He would, for instance, expect his subordinates to address him as "His Excellency," or "Honorable." He wasn't oyinbo-ish, though. He couldn't afford to be, once he decided to run for office. He had his colleagues, constituents, sponsors and godfathers who wouldn't stand for that, and had to be careful not to offend them as he set about enriching himself. There had always been rumors that he had affairs with women Busola would deem local. A few years back, he got a blogger locked up for posting a story about him fathering the son of an Abuja runs girl, until the story was retracted with an apology. Busola stayed married to him, regardless, even as they began to live apart. She was either in Lagos, at their Ikoyi house, or in London, where they had a flat in Knightsbridge. He was in Abuja or in his hometown, where he was granted a chieftaincy title.

Perhaps out of loneliness, Busola often entertains guests at home. She invites Enitan to lunch on Sunday, but Enitan, who works a sixty-hour week, if she factors in her commute to her office, is choosy about what she does in her spare time. She has run out of excuses for avoiding Busola, so is pleased to say she'll be with her father.

"Oh," Busola says. "That's all right, then. I called on the off chance you'd be free. It's just a small gathering of friends."

Enitan attended a dinner party at Busola's house with such a gathering last year and pictures her as she was—welcoming smile, makeup professionally done, bob wig, black adirẹ boubou with scarlet embroidery, and chrome-silver nails. Her dinner party was the usual spectacle of merriment seen at similar functions in Lagos. There was too much to eat and too much to drink. Wale, who was home for once, resurrected a bottle of vintage cognac from what looked like a miniature casket as Busola joked about her cook's Nigerian version of ratatouille, which she called rata-stewy.

The Aderemis' house is a charming, restored colonial one-story with a front yard, where a row of pine trees stand. Indoors, their paintings are collector's pieces, their furniture is from Milan and their floor tiling is by artisans from Cotonou. Busola has great taste and is a superb hostess, but Enitan can't bear the thought of having lunch with her and her friends. She can't even think of anyone close to her who understands why she remains in contact with Busola.

Niyi despised her when they were neighbors on Sunrise Estate. Sheri found her perplexing, and Ladi had no patience for her affectations when he met her. He refused to go to her dinner party, saying, "No, no, no," as if one "no" wasn't enough. Surprisingly, only Yimika could see why Enitan would spend time with Busola, though her reasoning was flawed. She was friends with Busola's children and familiar with her ways. "Mum," she said, without malice, when Enitan was hesitant about going to the dinner party, "it's like a reality show at the Aderemis'. Go and you'll feel better about yourself after you leave." Enitan didn't feel better about herself. She only felt complicit.

She asks after Busola's daughter, Toriola, and her son, Tomisin, to divert the conversation. They both have law degrees from English universities but are not interested in practicing law. Toriola has a brand of urban wear, which she sells online, and Tomisin is a rap artist. They stay at their parents' flat in Knightsbridge.

"Tori's just come out with a new range of T-shirts," Busola says, "and Tomi's finally working on an album."

"Wow," Enitan says. "That's great."

She was shocked when Yimika told her what Tomisin was doing after he graduated. "He went to Winchester," she said. "What's there to rap about? School rules?" Yimika said, "Come on, Mum. He won't be the first posh kid to act street." Toriola was just as confusing. All those years at Wycombe Abbey and she spoke with an affected South London accent. The last time Enitan saw them, Toriola had a septum nose ring and Tomisin's neck was covered in tattoos. They were confident, engaging and polite, but she did wonder what their parents thought, after making sure they'd been to the right schools.

"I'm trying to persuade them to come home," Busola says.

"That would be nice," Enitan says.

"Yes. Enough of the expat life. I told them they can continue what they're doing right here. So watch out. I'll be launching Fashion and Music Box soon."

Busola's PR firm is called Box, underneath which she has Art Box, Book Box and Film Box. Enitan had assumed artists tried to avoid boxes, but Busola has built up a client roster that includes ladies who launch in the arts. Enitan is on her mailing list, so she is vaguely aware of what they get up to. They wear outfits that suggest they are bohemian by Lagos standards, and call themselves curators, publishers and producers. Once in a while, they dabble in creative endeavors like putting together coffee-table books. They are basically dilettantes, and their launches are a new form of owambẹ party. They show off to their guests and Busola does her best to make them look cultured. She has always been inventive, especially when it comes to supporting her family. She ran a Montessori school when her children were young and got a Bachelor of Arts in public relations while they were in boarding school, just in time for Wale's senatorial campaign. She is well placed to promote them.

"How's Yimi finding Lagos?" Busola asks.

"She loves it," Enitan says. "She's heading back to London next month, though."

"I'm sure you'll miss her. She's such a lovely girl, Yimi. Such a lovely girl."

Enitan asks after Busola's brother and sister, Kayode and Ronke.

"I told you how Kay treated me," Busola says.

"Yes," Enitan says, soberly.

"Well, he hasn't apologized, and until he does, I'm not visiting him."

Kayode lives in London with his English wife, Portia, and they stay at the Chelsea flat. Portia runs an online eco-tourism company from it while Kayode keeps lying about his career.

He lied that he was an investment banker, then he lied that he was a hedge fund manager. Perhaps he wasn't having any success applying for City jobs. He was sixty-one, a chartered accountant and so oyinbo-ish it would never occur to him to return to Nigeria. His parents gave up on him. For years, he was getting by as a senior manager in a firm, where he had no prospects of becoming a partner, until he was laid off. Busola went to the flat to see him last year and he got so angry when she said he was unemployed that he stomped to the front door, opened it wide and ordered her to get out.

"Ron's okay," Busola continues. "She's finally getting help at a new center."

"Thank God," Enitan says, sincerely.

"I told you she was going to church for a while."

"You did."

"Such a waste of time."

Ronke's story was heartbreaking. She, too, had mingled with the High Socs in London, but the guys expected their girlfriends to look good and keep their mouths shut. Busola couldn't manage the latter, which was why she dated an English copywriter she met on the job until her parents found out and threatened to disown her if she didn't come back to Nigeria immediately.

Ronke was the sort of girl that High Soc guys took possession of. She was pretty, demure and had that diminutive stature they favored. All she needed to do was show up at a party and they would surround her. She was only in her first year in university when she started dating a guy who drove a Porsche and had a reputation for snorting cocaine. She was studying political science and he, economics. His father was a member of Annabel's and Elephant on the River, so they would frequent places like that. The awful guy was beating her all along and continued to do so after they returned to Lagos and got married. Each time, Ronke would escape to her parents' house on Queen's Drive. Her father would beg her to leave him, and her mother would urge her to go back to him. She then got hooked on valium and her husband, who had kicked his cocaine habit by then, filed for a divorce on the grounds that he couldn't have children with her until she'd cleaned up. Ronke never recovered. She moved in with her parents and started going to a megachurch for counselling. Her pastor convinced her that she had a generational curse, which she could break by praying.

"I don't know what she and Kay would do if the Lagos house and London flat weren't in my mother's name," Busola says. "I

Indigene

mean, they have enough from our father's estate to sustain them, but it's been so divvied up."

Enitan doesn't comment, but she is aware of the background story. Busola's father and mother were clients of her father's and he handled their wills. Busola's mother left the two properties to her children and her father's estate was shared by his two families.

Enitan attended his wake with her father five years ago. Busola sat with Wale and their children on one side. Ronke was in the middle with their mother. On the other side of them were Kayode, Portia and their three sons, who had cornrows. They were all in navy-blue aṣọ ẹbi, and poor Portia kept checking her auto-gele to make sure it wasn't slipping off. Enitan expressed her condolences to Kayode, after her father did, and Kayode thanked her and mumbled, "They never learn." Enitan walked on, wondering who he was referring to until it occurred to her that it was probably his father, whose other family were in purple aṣọ ẹbi. No one was surprised or scandalized, except by the fact that the families openly ignored each other.

Their father was an Otunba, and he was given the title in the early eighties, when being a chief wasn't enough, even as some of them created the title Double Chief to separate themselves from the rest. Various chiefs, ọtunbas, ọbas and other traditional rulers showed up for his wake. So did former and current politicians and civil servants. An ex-president praised him for being a patriarch, industrialist and philanthropist.

Enitan was in two minds about Busola's father. She'd taken a liking to him because he was fun. Whenever he visited her father in Lagos, he would laugh from the moment he walked into the house to the moment he left. Busola's mother, on the other hand, always looked thoroughly miserable when Enitan saw her at the Chelsea flat. She would greet her and stay out of her way. She started seeing Busola's father in another light only after her father was released from detention. He was one of those who avoided her father, and she suspected they were disappointed in him for defending a rabble-rouser like Mukoro.

She had terrible thoughts at the wake. Thoughts she couldn't help but have while watching the procession of VIP guests. She realized she was witnessing the demise of an era of Radio men who were called patriarchs, industrialists and philanthropists. Men who created nothing that hadn't existed before. Men who gave nothing, except a fraction of what they'd taken. Men who stood for nothing, even though they'd capitalized on the independence and pro-democracy movements. Businesspeople were no longer fooled by their success. TVs were busy defaulting on loans, forex round-tripping and doing whatever it took to be the next dollar billionaires. Internets looked up to the likes of Gates, Bezos, Zuckerberg and Musk, which was another matter. She came to the conclusion that the only effect that trickled down from men like Busola's father was their behavior. If she saw someone run a red light and try to escape a fine, she blamed them. If she saw someone jump a queue, she ascribed it to them. If she read about anyone who has extorted, embezzled or laundered money it was them, them, them. All that type of behavior was due to them because everyone wanted to be like them.

Busola's father was quickly forgotten by society, and his wife later developed Alzheimer's. Ronke lived with her until she died, and that was a particularly difficult time for Busola. Their mother would praise Ronke for being a good daughter and curse her for being neglectful. She got some respite when their mother couldn't recognize either of them and stopped talking altogether. That was why Enitan stayed in touch with Busola. She knew what it was like for her to have a difficult relationship with her parents.

"I hear sixty's the new sexy," Busola says.

Enitan laughs. "I don't know about that. All I've been doing so far is taking stock."

"Yes? Of what?"

"Where I am. Where I've been."

"Taking stock," Busola murmurs. "I should try that sometime."

"Only if you need to."

"We all need to. Think about what we've been through. People assume our lives have been easy. They don't know. They have no idea. Money isn't everything. Look at our families. Our fathers really messed us and our mothers up."

We. Our. Us. This is why Enitan avoids Busola. She demands loyalty from people she considers part of her group of friends. So do they. They don't forgive anyone who abandons or betrays them, so Enitan at times has to belong.

"Things were different then," she says. "Now, we'd be lucky if our children considered us good parents."

"True," Busola says. "Anyway, I just thought I'd try and get you to join us."

"Thanks for thinking of me," Enitan says. "Sorry I can't make it."

"Not to worry," Busola says. "Maybe next time."

Ladi is happy to hear that Enitan isn't going to Busola's house, for medical reasons. They have dinner at a Chinese restaurant on Victoria Island two days after the World Health Organization declares COVID-19 a pandemic.

"She's just flown in from London," he says. "You never know. We have to start taking this virus seriously. People abroad are social distancing and Italy is on lockdown."

Enitan isn't overly concerned. Nigeria has twelve confirmed cases of COVID-19, according to him, but it is Friday the 13th and she is superstitious.

"Please don't jinx us," she says.

"Okay," he says, resignedly.

She visits her father on Sunday and finds him alone in his sitting room. Auntie Simi is at her grandson's tenth birthday party, and for the first time Enitan considers the impact of a COVID-19 spread in Lagos before surrendering the thought.

Her father says he heard from Grace Ameh, who invited them to her book launch which he and Auntie Simi won't be able to attend.

"I haven't heard from her in years," Enitan says.

Grace is now an editor of *The Daily Recorder*, an online newspaper, and she writes a weekly column that Enitan reads occasionally, despite being put off by the number of pop-up ads.

The last time they saw each other was at a ten-year memorial service for Peter Mukoro in Lagos. His wife, Clara, was there with their children. So were former employees of his defunct magazine, *Oracle*, and members of the women's group that Grace formed to petition General Abacha's regime to release her detained colleagues. Her book is a biography of Mukoro titled *Son of the Soil*, which is fitting. He was the son of an Urhobo farmer and had spent most of his life suing the government and oil companies that destroyed his father's land before he got caught up in the pro-democracy movement.

"When is the launch?" Enitan asks.

"Today."

"Today!"

Her father eyes her. "Ehen?"

Enitan lowers her voice. "You didn't mention it before."

"You think my memory is as it used to be?"

"You've never complained."

Her father shrugs. "It's a useful impairment. There are a few things I'd like to forget, or claim I've forgotten."

Enitan takes a breath. "I should try and go. Where is it, please?"

"Freedom Park."

"What time, please?"

"Four to six, she says, and there will be a reception afterwards."

Freedom Park is not too far from Enitan's office, but from her father's house it will take about an hour to get there, even on a Sunday.

"I might be able to make it for the reception," she says.

Her father nods. "That would be good. At least I will be represented."

Enitan gives him a mock-weary look, which he ignores.

She leaves his house earlier than usual. On her way to Freedom Park, she passes Tafawa Balewa Square, which was called Lagos Race Course when Nigeria's independence was celebrated there on October the 1st, 1960. She drives up Campbell Street, passing Lagos Island Maternity Hospital, where she was born; Bola Chemist, a pharmacy her mother used; and Saint Nicholas Hospital, where her brother was often admitted for treatment. The park is on the grounds of a former colonial prison known as Her Majesty's Broad Street Prisons. Nationalist politicians like

Herbert Macaulay and Obafemi Awolowo were once held there. Parts of the old walls have been preserved, as have a few of the original almond and breadfruit trees. These days, the park hosts cultural festivals, music concerts, art exhibitions, plays, readings and book launches. But it is state government property, so there are limits to freedom of expression there.

Enitan arrives at six thirty as the sun begins to set. The gateman gives her directions to the venue of the launch, and she hurries along to a one-story building, in front of which is a paved food court. A number of people sit at plastic tables, eating and drinking as Afropop plays. A poster of Fela leans against the outdoor stairs that lead to the venue. Enitan walks up them, glancing at a wall mural of a woman hugging herself. It is a project for the Girl Child Art Foundation and under it is a statement on the Campaign for Sexual and Reproductive Rights that she doesn't stop to read.

She enters a lounge which has several round glass tables and red chairs. On either side of it are tinted sliding windows. Only a handful of people are present—Grace, Clara and other guests she doesn't recognize. Grace wears an indigo adirẹ boubou and head tie, and Clara is in royal-blue traditional Urhobo attire. Enitan approaches them and they both shout her name in surprise. She hugs them and apologizes for being late. They appear to be in good spirits, despite the usual wear and tear. Clara has shadows around her eyes, and Grace's hair is faded gray. Out of respect for their ages, Enitan doesn't call them by their first names, even though Clara once ordered her to.

Grace begins to scold her immediately after their greetings.

"You," she says, pointing at Enitan. "I'm quarrelling with you. What is this? You don't even ask about me anymore."

Indigene

Enitan laughs. "I do!"

Grace wags her finger. "No, you don't. Only Uncle Sunny asks about me."

"Am I not here?" Enitan asks, turning to Clara.

"Don't mind her," Clara says to Enitan, narrowing her eyes. "If you know what she put me through over this book, disturbing me from morning till night. You handle her. Me, I'm going to my house."

"It is well," Grace says, rubbing her hands together innocently.

After Clara leaves, Enitan buys three copies of Mukoro's biography, which has a portrait photo of him on the cover, his smile and moustache like Omar Sharif's. For all his journalistic integrity, he was a chronic womanizer, but Clara reconciled herself to that. She once described him as a boy running around a sweet shop.

Grace signs the books with personalized messages before she and Enitan sit at a table, where they drink cold water out of mini plastic bottles.

"Sorry I can't offer you something more," Grace says. "We ran out of refreshments and our guests went to the food court. We could go there if you prefer."

"This is fine," Enitan says.

The music is less obtrusive upstairs. The lyrics of the current Afropop track are in pidgin and the singer brags about buying designer wear and luxury cars.

"Where's your husband?" Grace asks.

"Playing golf," Enitan says, putting her bottle down. "We're not married, though."

Grace frowns. "Still? Why not?"

Enitan raises her hands. "Just like that."

"I'm a romantic at heart."

Enitan smiles. "So am I. Is Mr. Ameh around?"

"He left. You know he's never had time for me and my Aluta comrades."

"Is that what he calls them?"

Grace nods. "You included."

Enitan shakes her head. She was no Aluta, but joining the group was probably her most significant accomplishment as a lawyer. She can't say for sure that the letters they wrote to Abacha's regime secured the release of her father, Mukoro and others, but she appreciates the irony of a women's group campaigning for the rights of men. Grace's husband, Joe, was initially resistant to the group, but he eventually came round and was named an honorary woman.

"How are things at *The Daily Recorder*?" Enitan asks.

"All right," Grace says. "But it's not like working for *Oracle*."

"What are your former colleagues up to now?"

"Some are in journalism and others are in public relations or jobs that pay better. Two are at *TDR* with me."

TDR is known for investigative journalism. It covers religious violence and terrorism in Northern Nigeria and in the Middle Belt region, where Grace is from. Ethnic tensions have been an undertow since the civil war, so *TDR* also reports on regional separatist movements like Oduduwa Republic in the South West, the Indigenous People of Biafra in the South East, and the Movement for the Emancipation of the Niger Delta in the South South.

In her column, Grace writes mostly about matters pertaining to Nigerian youth, such as Academic Staff Union of Universities strikes and the japa syndrome. Now and again she gives her take on legal cases that make national headlines. Last year, there was Blessing's case, another about a pastor who allegedly raped a church worker and yet another about school bullies who tormented and killed a younger student. Grace felt they were compromised by media attention. She often courts controversy with her scathing columns on international personalities during their official visits to Nigeria. She argued that Christine Lagarde was as much a danger to African women as Dominique Strauss-Kahn for championing neoliberal economic policies.

"How are things at Taiwo and Associates?" she asks.

"The same," Enitan says. "I spend too much time editing briefs, but hopefully we'll resolve that this year."

"Editing is my whole life. What about Indigene?"

Enitan is reluctant to talk about Indigene, but she tells Grace about her dilemma and inability to make a decision.

"I'm not surprised," Grace says. "Activism is over in Nigeria."

"You think so?"

"I know so."

"Why are Nigerians quick to call themselves activists, then?"

"They're trying to fool themselves, or other people."

"I pretty much said the same about a feminist group here and wondered if I was being harsh. My daughter thinks my views are too rigid. You know young people."

Grace wrinkles her nose. "They don't value parental advice and I don't blame them."

"I was the same. They can be inspiring, though. She cares about the environment."

"Which one? Overseas or here?"

Enitan laughs. "Aren't they all connected?"

"If that's the case, viruses are more of a threat right now."

"Hm."

They drink more water, Grace finishing her bottle and setting it aside.

"You're not being harsh," she says. "We have imposters everywhere."

Enitan widens her eyes. "Even in the arts!"

Grace nods. "They've infiltrated the arts pages, and they pay my colleagues to praise them and celebrate their mediocrity. Festival organizers who collect money from corrupt politicians. Producers who fund projects that pander to them. The other day I found out that a playwright, who is making the rounds in Europe and America, got unknown women to write her play and stripped them of rights, yet she calls herself a feminist."

"Na wa."

"Most of them are self-serving. They complain about patriarchy in Nigeria, but globalization affects them more. The pressure to be seen, heard and succeed globally. Their lives improve as other Nigerian women's lives remain the same or get worse. If their organizations were independently audited, I'm sure the audits would uncover fraud. Men, too, are now jumping on the bandwagon to get a piece of the pie. I heard about one who set up a domestic violence shelter with his wife, and started begging foreign donors for money, yet he was beating her up at home."

"Oh dear."

"There is a market for ideas abroad, that's all, and where there's a market, Nigerians will find a product to sell. Identity politics is the latest one."

"How come people abroad don't know when they're being hustled?"

Indigene

"They know. They don't care so long as they can sell an African. They want us to worship individualism as much as they do, even though they've seen the disharmony it causes. But let's focus on what we are doing here. If you look at the system as a whole, you will understand why you can't function as an activist within it. First, money has overtaken morality."

"Totally."

"It doesn't matter who we are or where we're coming from, there isn't a single aspect of our lives that hasn't been affected. Secondly, there has been a complete breakdown of public education."

"Complete and utter."

"Parents, who can afford to, send their children to the few private educational institutions we have or they send them overseas."

"These are the options."

"I went to Lekki to research a story I was working on about a school there, and the number of school signs I saw with the word 'British' in them, one would think I was somewhere in England."

When Grace opens her mouth, no one is spared, not even Grace herself, so there's no use lying.

"My daughter went to one before she went to England."

"You see?"

"Our best graduates japa, anyway."

"To become what? Spare blacks?"

Enitan laughs. "Oh my goodness!"

"I'm not joking," Grace says. "Clara and I have seven children and ten grandchildren between us and not one of them lives in Nigeria. Her youngest son has just moved to Australia."

"Australia, ke?"

"Yes. He married an Australian woman and we thank God they're happy together. But is it fair that we don't see our families overseas unless they buy us plane tickets to visit them?"

"Not at all."

"Oh-ho. And it's from the Middle Belt down we're seeing this pattern. Northerners don't japa as Southerners do, even though they have the highest rate of illiteracy and are at the mercy of Almajiri education. We'll see how that plays out in years to come."

Enitan shakes her head. "Nigeria."

"Blessed country. Blessed. What don't we have? Natural resources. Resilient and hardworking people. It's shameful what is going on. Our youth are seventy percent of our population and we can't give them decent educations. We don't teach history in schools anymore, and we sit back and watch as they imbibe whatever is happening overseas, then we wonder why we're losing our culture. Most of them don't follow the news, even when it's online. Instead, they follow celebrity gossip, reality shows and influencers—"

"Influencers."

"The sort who won't say anything that will impact their brands negatively, and Afropop artists who keep them in a trance." Grace gestures at the window as the latest track pays tribute to Nigerian businessmen who are dollar billionaires. "You hear that? If they listened to Fela's Afrobeat half as much, their heads would be correct by now. They would march to that House of Assembly, surround the whole place and refuse to leave until their demands are met."

Enitan remembers student demonstrations in the seventies and eighties that ended in bloodshed, like the Ali Must Go and

Ango Must Go protests. She would never advise young Nigerians to risk their lives that way. For what? So the government can call them rioters? So the army and police can shoot them dead and deny killing them? So they can become forgotten heroes? No. She would rather they remain Internet warriors. While they're at it, they can stay out of jail by not making statements that could be deemed unlawful.

"What do you think of online activism?" she asks.

"I've seen causes take hold," Grace says. "But how many Nigerians have access to the Internet? The question is this—If we could challenge a military dictatorship, why are we unable to do the same with a democratically elected government?"

Enitan looks Grace in the eye. "We're complacent and complicit."

Grace shrugs. "Because of their methods of suppressing us. The military and the politicians use force and collusion to rule. But the military relies on force, which eventually leads to a pushback. Politicians rely on collusion. They collude with people in the civil service, police, army, law courts and media. Add the churches and mosques they donate money to for votes."

"Add the banks that fund their campaigns, launder their loot, and channel a little of it into corporate social responsibility events."

"You get the picture? This is why young Nigerians prepare to japa as if they're planning prison escapes. As for those who stay on, I pray we don't end up with a Pied Piper who will play to them and lead them astray. Politicians are not interested in dismantling the system. They just want to win and uphold it. If you're an activist, you will end up discredited and arrested. They will Sowore you if you so much as say the word 'revolution.' Any activist that can function in a system like this is no more than paid or controlled opposition. Believe it."

"And restructuring? What do you think of it?"

"Well . . . Nigeria was created as a company to benefit its founders and shareholders in Britain. Independence extended shares to a limited number of us, but every other Nigerian was expected to work for the company. Restructuring will only extend shares to those who engineer it. To me, the only solution is to dissolve the company and establish cooperatives."

"What, socialism?"

"I call it a return to an indigenous system that served us well."

"It's too late for that. Capitalism is in our blood."

"It's in the blood of our founders and shareholders. I'm looking ahead anyway. You and I will be long gone."

"It won't work, Mrs. Ameh."

"Is what we have now working?"

Enitan could challenge Grace based on current evidence. Every institution with a socialist bent fails the general public. She doesn't have an alternative solution, though. She has a suggestion—that Nigerians redirect the time they spend discussing the problems of Nigeria towards making sure their governments serve them well. She has a prediction that anarchy will be the end result of the course Nigeria is on. But both are obvious.

"This is why Mr. Ameh calls you an Aluta," she says.

Grace points at her. "You, too, are one. I recognize Alutas when I see them. He says we're pessimists, but I say we're optimists. Anyone who is satisfied with where Nigeria is today can't have hope."

Enitan smiles. Nothing that Grace has said is news to her, but Grace's affirmation helps her to accept that she has to continue Indigene as a charity. She doesn't know why she didn't think of speaking to her first. She rarely disagrees with her columns. She is only more inclined to reflect on other people's opinions and her doubts.

Grace sits back in her chair. "When is your next visit to Kirikiri?"

"April."

"That's around the corner. We'll be on lockdown by then."

"That soon?"

Grace nods. "It is inevitable, the way COVID is spreading overseas. You won't be able to go anywhere if that happens. Maybe then we will be forced to sit at home and take a closer look at our lives."

"Maybe."

"Who knows? It might even force the prisons to release more detainees."

Enitan sighs. "That would be one good thing to come out of it."

She talks to Grace until the sun has almost set. Before she leaves, she sends WhatsApp messages to Ladi and Yimika about her decision on Indigene. Ladi replies with a brown thumbs-up emoji and Yimika with pink hearts. She replies to each of them with a throbbing red heart emoji and sends texts to her father and Sheri to inform them as well.

As she drives out of the park, she tells herself that she must pay more attention to the news about COVID-19. She can be detached and objective about death while handling her clients' affairs, but not in her private life. The likelihood of the pandemic spreading around Nigeria causes her to panic on her way to Marina Road. What will happen if Ladi contracts the virus? What will happen if her father or Yimika does? What will happen to them if she does? The implications are so overwhelming that she tunes out before she reaches her destination.

Her view of the waterfront is obscured by a brick wall until she ascends Five Cowries Creek Bridge and catches sight of Lagos harbor at twilight. An amber hue divides the indigo lagoon and sky. She takes this as a sign of the clarity she has been looking for as she descends the bridge.

On Ozumba Mbadiwe Avenue, she reaches a bottleneck and is able to check her mobile phone for text replies. Her father's reads, "I thought we already established this," and Sheri's asks, "What about the food packs?" She will call them at home. She must call Ladi, too. She also has to speak to Yimika about the possibility of staying on in Lagos, instead of returning to London in April. She definitely needs her advice about working online.

The traffic remains heavy to Lekki Toll Gate. By the time Enitan gets to Admiralty Way, it is night. Lit signs illuminate the street, which is congested with vehicles that make a din. She passes plants for sale, a bank, a gym, a pharmacy, a petrol station, a liquor store, a print and copy shop, a Mac center and Dulux center and her dry cleaner. Everywhere she looks, people are on the move—the usual pedestrians, commuters, traders and beggars—and at this hour they are joined by scantily dressed sex workers. She can't imagine commercial activity in Lagos coming to a halt in the event of a lockdown, or expecting its inhabitants to be more distant from each other than they are now.

UNSUITABLE TIES

She would rather not be here tonight. For her, a dinner party at a hotel—especially a five-star hotel like this in London—is research work. She might notice a seating-card design, a flower arrangement or some other catering idea she can use when she returns to Lagos. She will study the menu from hors d'oeuvres to desserts. As for the company, she knows what to expect: rich Nigerians, all connected to each other.

The hotel, Greek Revival style, is in Knightsbridge. It is cold for May, so she and her husband, Akin, wear coats, which they leave at the cloakroom near the lobby. The cloakroom attendant hands her a ticket and she puts it in her clutch bag. She is conscious of her heels clip-clopping along the marble-floored corridor that leads to the bar. At the entrance, a waiter lifts a silver tray with flutes of champagne and Buck's Fizz. She goes for the champagne, as does Akin. They thank the waiter, a woman.

The bar resembles a candle-lit library in a stately home. It has shelves of old, leather-bound books and maroon patterned wallpaper. Cocktails are at 7 PM, dinner is at 7:45 PM, followed by dancing. Carriages are at 1 AM. The dress code is black tie. Akin has decided that means he can get away with wearing a tie that is black.

She took the time and trouble to go from their flat in West Kensington to Kensington High Street to buy a new dress the day before. It was typical of Akin to forget he needed a bow tie until the last moment, yet he was the one who insisted that she come.

Other guests are on time. All are appropriately turned out, a few in colorful traditional Nigerian wear. She and Akin return their smiles and waves as they approach their host, Saheed Balogun.

"How now, my brother?" Saheed asks.

"Hey," Akin says, shaking Saheed's hand.

"Saheed," she says, with a nod.

Saheed looks as if he has only just recognized her. "Yemisi! Long time no see!"

She winces involuntarily as he hugs her. She has become used to seeing his face under newspaper headlines since his fraud investigation began a month ago. He was also recently listed in an online magazine as one of Nigeria's top ten billionaires. He is remarkably slight in person and sports a gray goatee. His bow tie is not quite as symmetrical after he hugs her. She was not expecting him to welcome her that way. Feeling hijacked, she looks around the bar and asks, "Where is Funke?"

"She's taking care of last-minute seating arrangements," Saheed says.

Yemisi grimaces. Nigerians don't always RSVP and sometimes show up with extra guests. Funke is Saheed's wife. Yemisi might call her an old friend, though she is more accurately someone Yemisi socialized with when they were both law undergrads. Funke was at University of Lagos while she was at University College London. Their paths often crossed in Lagos and London. For reasons she can't explain, she doesn't mind Funke, but she absolutely cannot stand Saheed.

She leaves Akin with him. She told Akin she intended to stay as far away from Saheed as possible. That was the condition on which she came.

The Balogun's dinner party is one in a series of fiftieth birthday parties that she and Akin have attended outside Nigeria, given by Nigerians. There have been several in London, and destination parties elsewhere. One in Cape Town, another in Dubai, and yet another, much talked about and blogged about, on the French Riviera, which they missed. At the end of May, Funke is having a more intimate party in St. Kitts. They will skip that as well. On Funke's actual birthday, which is at the end of June, she will finish with a masked ball in Lagos, in the Civic Centre Grand Banquet Hall. Saheed is flying in a seventies American funk band for that. Why such a blatant display of wealth when he is being investigated by the Economic and Financial Crimes Commission, Yemisi cannot understand.

She circulates, champagne flute in one hand, clutch bag in the other, greeting friends, curtsying for elders and laughing. She is astonished at her capacity to look as if she is enjoying herself. She can't believe the people who have shown up, despite Saheed's investigation—legal people, church people. There is a former state attorney general she attended law school with, and a Pentecostal church pastor she had a crush on in her teens, one summer in Lagos when they took tennis lessons at Ikoyi

Club. Funke is a member of his church. Saheed is Muslim, but he attends church services now and then. Through Funke, the pastor apparently receives a fee for praying for Saheed's business, and ten percent of his profits.

Yemisi doesn't have any clients in the bar. She usually gets work through her connections with the banking crowd in Lagos. Akin has a private equity firm and his clients are senators, governors and government ministers, former and incumbent. Only to her would he admit they are a bunch of thieves. His wealthiest clients, like Saheed, are in the petroleum industry. He sometimes refers to them as oil money.

A waiter approaches her with a tray of vol-au-vents and she tucks her bag under her arm. She chooses one with chicken and mushroom filling and thanks him. Most of the waiters are English, but some look as if they are from other countries in Europe. They are friendly yet unobtrusive and poised without being snooty. They go about their business as if they're with their regular clientele. They've probably been briefed on how to handle the Nigerian function. She thinks of her waiters back home, who would be timid around Nigerians like these. She often tells them they are working, not asking for favors, but they ignore her or laugh at her.

The vol-au-vent is perfectly light. She is eating it when Oyinda and her husband, Oliver, walk in.

"Hello, darling," Oyinda says.

"Sorry," Yemisi mumbles. "My . . . mouth . . . is . . . full."

She dabs the corner of her mouth with her napkin in a mock-ladylike manner.

Oyinda is in a short, black dress and her hair is cropped and natural. She wears no makeup, as usual, but her nails are painted lilac.

She points at Akin. "I see we're not the only ones wearing unsuitable ties."

"It was a struggle," Yemisi says.

"Mine thinks bow ties are silly," Oyinda says.

"Bow ties *are* silly," Oliver says.

His English accent makes him sound ruder. He is blond with thick-rimmed glasses and an overly serious expression. His suit and tie are mod. Yemisi remembers when Nigerians, out of laziness, described him as "that punk rocker guy." She has never known if Oyinda drifted away from other Nigerians, or if it was the other way around, because she married Oliver.

"How are your parents coping with retirement?" Oyinda asks.

"Quite well," Yemisi says. "And yours?"

"Oh, my mother's still working. Yes, she's still going strong. She's not as active as she used to be, but she will attend a conference when she can. My father, on the other hand . . ." Oyinda pulls a face. "He's busy golfing or doing whatever else he does. What about your kids? They must be out of their teens now."

"My daughter is," Yemisi says. "My son's eighteen."

She and Oyinda met when they were thirteen. There were not many Nigerian students in English boarding schools back then. Her school was in Canterbury, Kent, and Oyinda's was somewhere in Dorset. Their parents made them go to the cinema together during an Easter holiday in London. Oyinda was one of those students who just never returned to Nigeria. She is a pediatrician now, and a Fellow of the Royal College of

Paediatrics and Child Health. Oliver is a photographer, and brilliant, apparently. They have no children. They ski and hike together. Their last trip was a sponsored climb up Kilimanjaro to raise money for a medical cause that benefited African children.

"How's Lagos treating you these days?" Oyinda asks.

"You don't want to know," Yemisi says.

"Go on," Oyinda urges. "Tell me."

Yemisi rambles on about her life on Lekki Peninsula. Armed robberies are rare, the main streets are fairly clean, but the side streets get waterlogged during the rainy season. The traffic is getting worse, there was a petrol shortage before she traveled and still no regular electricity. She had to buy a new electricity generator for her catering kitchen because her old one broke down.

Oyinda exclaims, "Oh no," over and over, her voice getting higher, until it drops in a confession: "That's why I can't live there."

"We're luckier than most," Yemisi says. "And at least we get to escape once in a while."

She can't complain further. She and Akin live in a serviced estate, so they have constant electricity and running water. Their home is a four-bedroom house with boys' quarters, where their house help stay during the week. Their drivers live elsewhere.

Oyinda widens her eyes. "Did you read the article in which Saheed was mentioned?"

"What article?"

"The one about the one percent in Lagos."

"Oh, that."

Oyinda shakes her head. "So embarrassing. So, so embarrassing."

"Yes, it was."

Unsuitable Ties

For a moment Yemisi thought Oyinda was referring to Saheed's EFCC investigation. Nigeria itself has been in the international news of late, and not in flattering ways. There was the article about the one percent in Lagos, which appeared in an American newspaper, followed by another in a British glossy magazine about spoiled, rich Nigerian students in London. Two Christmases ago there was the underwear bomber, who was ridiculed back home for being privileged, above all else. For years there have been reports on Boko Haram attacks in Northern Nigeria, and this January there was the Occupy Nigeria movement.

"It was a hatchet job," Oyinda says. "I mean, some of us work hard for a living. We're not all flying around in private jets and lounging on yachts."

"I know, I know," Yemisi says.

She would say the article lacked perspective, but foreign press coverage of Nigeria often does. She dismissed the piece. It wasn't worth her energy to take umbrage as a Nigerian who lived overseas might.

"Mind you," Oyinda whispers, "some of this lot here..."

Yemisi blinks slowly. She gossips only at home. Oyinda has a reputation for gossiping anywhere and without discretion.

She can see why Oyinda thinks she is part of the one percent in Lagos, even though Oyinda doesn't live there. Oyinda would think she belongs because she comes from what Yemisi's mother would call a good family, based there. Fathers' illustrious careers count, mothers' less so. Oyinda's father was a First Republic health minister and one of the top gynecologists in Lagos of his time. He was also notorious for having affairs with his nurses, for which Oyinda has never forgiven him. But Lagos has since changed. Talking about backgrounds will only get laughs. All it takes to belong to the one percent is money. The Baloguns belong by virtue of the billions of naira Saheed receives from the government as fuel-subsidy payments to import petroleum products. The EFCC investigation is to determine if his company actually does import petroleum products or if it exists solely to collect the subsidy payments.

"This party must be costing a fortune," Oyinda says.

Yemisi raises her hand. "I'm not saying a word."

People trust her as if she were a doctor. She and Akin could easily be mistaken for being part of the one percent in Lagos, but she would say they live off them, by providing services, that they have to be useful to belong, and they also have to be loyal.

Oliver finally smiles, though conspiratorially. Perhaps he takes a while to warm up in company, as she does. Or perhaps he feels outnumbered. So far he is the only foreign guest. Whatever the reason, Yemisi has seen his photos of their Kilimanjaro trip on Facebook, and Oyinda, the only African besides their guide, was smiling away.

She excuses herself, trying to figure out how Oyinda knows the Baloguns. They are definitely not Oyinda's friends, but she would come to their party anyway, out of homesickness or curiosity. They would invite Oyinda because she is the sort of Nigerian they admire. Her mother, a public-health specialist, is a descendant of Lagos royalty. Her mother's father was a lawyer, her paternal grandfather was a politician, and his father was a publisher. She has generations of family history on both sides, recorded history, which is uncommon. The Baloguns would approve of her as a guest. They don't have social functions; they have social agendas.

Unsuitable Ties

Akin is still with Saheed. He leans in to listen to whatever Saheed is saying. Yemisi can tell from his discreet expression that they are discussing business. Could Saheed possibly be trying to invest more money with him at a time like this? She would have to find out. She would have to put a stop to that.

A waiter approaches her with a tray of canapés, and she again tucks her bag under her arm. She chooses one with smoked salmon and cream cheese, eats it and finishes her champagne.

She met Akin at Cambridge. They got their master's degrees in law there. They gave up law for banking when the banking sector was privatized in the eighties. Akin joined a commercial bank in Lagos where everyone went by their first names. She joined a merchant bank as a company secretary. They got married after Akin was appointed managing director. She left banking before he did to start her catering business; their children were in primary school, and she could no longer cope with her long working hours. Akin's parents were retired high court judges. They lived in Lagos, so they would sometimes babysit. She was never comfortable with relying on his parents. Her parents lived in the federal capital, Abuja. Her father was a retired diplomat and her mother, who throughout her father's career had hosted cocktail parties and dinner parties in Bonn, Paris and London, on a Nigerian budget, would describe herself as a housewife.

She and Akin were children of civil servants whose net worth shrank during the Structural Adjustment Program of the eighties, so they had to be ambitious. She has her father to thank for not turning out like other diplomats' children, who ended up shell-shocked in Nigeria after their fathers retired from the service, going on about the lives they used to have overseas. Whenever she asked her father for money, no matter how little, he would reply, "You think I'm rich?" She credits her mother for getting her into catering. As a girl, she would sulk whenever her mother called her to help in the kitchen. Her brothers never had to help. Her mother, worried Yemisi would turn out to be a useless wife, encouraged her to take a cordon bleu cookery course during her father's posting to London, which she unexpectedly enjoyed. That was when she realized she didn't actually hate cooking; she just wanted to get paid for it.

Akin earns more than she does. He always has. Their daughter is a junior at the University of Pennsylvania, studying economics. Their son wants to go to Imperial College London to study engineering. With foreign-student fees to pay, and a house in Lagos and flat in London to maintain, what else is Akin supposed to do but keep the money coming?

He is talking to Saheed now and she is sure he is making a pitch. After twenty-two years of marriage, she is past arguing about matters they can't resolve. There was a time they argued about his habit of procrastinating, his reluctance to do his small share of chores at home and his presumption that he was in charge of their children's education. These days, they have more than enough help at home, and they are lucky if their children listen to them. Akin still procrastinates, but he has that pitiful look good men develop when they've been nagged too long, not that different from the expression of a knackered horse. She is trying to be a nicer wife now, so she gives him breaks, but this is one quarrel they revisit as they go from one function to the next: his financial dealings with dubious clients like Saheed.

"Happy birthday to you," she sings, as Funke walks into the bar with Biola.

Funke feigns shyness. "None of that, please!"

"I beg you," Yemisi says to Biola. "Let me hug the celebrant first. I'll get to you next."

She hugs Funke and tells her she looks radiant because she can't think of a more suitable word. Funke is in a gold-lamé maxi dress, which must be custom-made. She is all diamonds from her décolletage up. She has a long hairweave and a thick layer of bronze eyeshadow that suggests she hired a makeup artist and dictated exactly how she wanted to look. She is pretty—much prettier without makeup.

"I've lost weight, haven't I?" Funke asks, posing.

"You never needed to," Yemisi says.

Funke often claims she is on a diet, though her appetite secretly remains healthy. Twice a year she disappears to a health spa in Spain for liquid detoxes and colonic irrigations. She bleaches her skin. That she can't hide. She also claims her complexion is the same as it has always been, but she was much darker before.

Metallic fabrics must be in. Biola is in a pewter-colored dress. Her black-pearl earrings match her dress, her short, bob wig is flattering and her makeup colors are neutral. She is naturally skinny, but may have had Botox work on her forehead. Yemisi suspects she deliberately tones down her appearance to make Funke look as if she is trying too hard.

"The lovely Mrs. Lawal," she says, hugging Biola tighter than she hugged Funke to make up for temporarily bypassing her. Biola is a family friend. Their mothers were childhood friends. Their fathers are die-hard Metropolitan Club men: any talk of allowing women to become members rubs them up the wrong way.

"How are Auntie and Uncle?" Biola asks.

"Very well," Yemisi says. "How's Chairman?"

"Chairman's fine," Biola says.

Everyone calls Biola's father Chairman. Biola's father calls himself an industrialist, to set himself apart from ordinary businessmen in Lagos. He has never manufactured a single product. He is chairman of several companies he acquired shares in before they became old and established.

Yemisi doesn't ask after Biola's stepmother. Biola's mother died when Biola was just ten and Chairman remarried—a glamorous Liberian divorcee, whom Biola refused to obey and called "the refugee" behind her back. When their rows got too much for Chairman, he sent Biola off to Le Rosey in Switzerland and gave her whatever she wanted to compensate for abandoning her. By the age of thirteen she was shopping on Bond Street. Chairman's only rule was that she study and pass her exams. Her stepmother hoped she might fail. Biola got into the London School of Economics to study law. After she graduated, she returned to Lagos for law school.

"So," Biola says, accusingly. "We only meet in London these days."

"Where else?" Yemisi says.

"You're a real socialite caterer, are you?"

"If you really mean I cater for socialites like you? Yes."

Biola laughs. She can't help but put another woman down, even in the course of saying hello.

The last place they met was in Lagos. They were at a barbecue on New Year's Day at Funke's house. Funke had waiters walking up and down with trays of jerk chicken, shrimp kebab and grilled tilapia. There were bottles of Moët rosé dripping on every table. Yemisi asked Funke who her caterer was and Funke said, "I flew in a chef from Senegal."

Biola arrived late that day with her ladies-in-waiting, a group of women who started the Birkin-bag trend in Lagos. Funke was also one of them. Yemisi would never cater for any of them. They would be too demanding. They would try to bully discounts out of her. They would never bother to return her phone calls or texts. If she persisted in trying to contact them, they would refer her to their personal assistants. They could end up mistreating her waiters, which would drive her up the wall. After the job was done, they would pay her in their own sweet time.

She looks forward to seeing Biola and Funke at functions anyway, knowing they will entertain her. She is particularly amused when they carry on as if Lagos and London are neighboring cities. "I'm going to London next week," Biola might say. "After which I come back to Lagos for a day, then I'm off again." Lagos is a mere six hours away by plane. They travel first class or business class.

The code of loyalty applies to them as well. Biola is married to Tunji Lawal, a senator who took a ten-billion-naira bank loan he never repaid. The EFCC investigated him, too. Funke said any rumors of financial impropriety on his part were a political vendetta. The EFCC eventually dropped their investigation. Funke again stood by Biola when Tunji's affair with a Lagos publicist was exposed. There were lewd text messages, which were quoted in the tabloids. There was a sex tape, which was posted online. Funke said the footage wasn't clear. The whole scandal made Yemisi more sympathetic toward Biola, who is now involved in eradicating poverty in Africa. She is invited around the world to give speeches. She is photographed with international celebrities and posts her photos on Facebook to spite her enemies.

Tunji is in Nigeria, attending a senators' forum. He is with the People's Democratic Party and still hopes to be president. Biola probably wouldn't mind being first lady, but meanwhile won't associate with the new crop of Fourth Republic politicians Tunji mixes with. She calls them bush people.

"Love your dress," Biola says. "Whose is it?"

"Who knows?" Yemisi says.

It is a pastel-blue maxi dress she bought on sale.

"She always looks good," Biola says to Funke.

"Where did you get it?" Funke asks.

"High Street Ken," Yemisi says.

"The color suits her," Biola says to Funke.

Yemisi wonders if her dress is worthy of this much attention or if it is just their acquisitive nature that gets the better of them. Perhaps they are mocking her, she thinks in amusement.

"It looks like a lawn van," Funke says.

"It doesn't look anything like a Lanvin," Biola says.

"It does. It looks like a lawn van dress I have."

"Lanvin is understated. You, my dear, are never understated."

"Have you seen their latest collection?"

"Excuse me," Yemisi says.

She hurries as if someone is calling her. There is only so much she can take when Funke and Biola begin to spar. Funke is the challenger here, and Biola is the undefeated and undisputed champion.

Biola has always been the champ. Funke may have had her moments of local glory: a fashion show, she is there in the front row; a Nollywood film premiere, she is on the red carpet as a producer. She is named in best-dressed lists. But only recently has she had international recognition, for building a world-class boutique hotel in Lagos. Saheed hired an American PR company to cover the opening and flew in the architect who designed the hotel, a Somali, highly celebrated in London. Saheed's billionaire status is most likely another PR stunt. Yet Biola wins every time because she gets Funke to up the ante. Biola has been making women feel small since she was a girl: her stepmother, her stepmother's friends, her friends' disapproving mothers. For her, this is sport.

Yemisi heads for the other end of the bar. She rarely sees either of them these days. She hears about them. Funke is considered a social climber and Biola an outright fraud. People get furious about her photos with international celebrities. Yemisi just wishes she could pull the celebrities aside and say, as her mother would, "Know the caliber of Nigerian you fraternize with."

They will pose with any African for a photo op. The gossip about Funke and Biola so far only makes her in awe of their ability to withstand it, though she imagines that in private, they are just as brutal about people who talk about them.

The bar empties a little after 7:45 PM. Yemisi guesses there are about a hundred guests in all. Oliver is no longer the only foreign guest. She passes a couple of men who sound German or Austrian. They must be Saheed's business partners.

On the pilgrimage to the dining room, she sidles up to Akin and whispers, "What were you and Saheed talking about?"

"When?" Akin asks.

"Keep your voice down, please."
"My voice is down."
"Lower it."
"Is this low enough?"
"For God's sake."

She walks ahead of Akin as he watches her with a bemused expression. His whispers are loud. Everyone around them will hear what he is saying.

Perhaps he has sold his soul to Saheed. Perhaps this is the man she married. Her clients are no different from his. She had one who bankrupted a finance house using an expense account before fleeing the country. She had another, a lovely woman, who would send her flowers after every catering job. The woman was frog-marched out of a bank when she was caught doing illegal foreign exchange deals. But she no longer caters for them.

She remembers when Saheed's name became the one to drop in Lagos. She asked Akin how Saheed made his money, and Akin said, "Why are you asking me?" Then Saheed became Akin's client, and Akin told her how, and she said, "Here we go again." There was oil in Nigeria, plenty of oil. In a normal country, there would probably be no need to import petroleum products. But the refineries in Nigeria didn't work, so the bulk of the oil was exported overseas and people like Saheed were in business.

She and Akin believed Saheed's business was bona fide back then, so she wasn't surprised Saheed had made his money overnight. She was just put off by how much he spent. When Akin told her Saheed was thinking of buying a yacht, she said she hoped Saheed could swim. When Akin mentioned that Saheed traveled to Monaco to watch the Grand Prix, she said if Saheed was interested in watching drivers trying to kill everyone in their way, he should have stayed in Lagos. Akin called her a snob. She didn't deny that. She got her snobbery from her mother. "He's so nouveau," she said. "We're all nouveau," Akin said.

The dining room has a marble fireplace, above which is a gilt-framed mirror. There are crystal chandeliers and period paintings of horses. The tables are beautifully set, but so far nothing inspires her. The designs are old and staid. Her clients want cutting-edge modern. She finds her name on the seating chart. She is at the same table as Funke and Biola. Shit, she thinks.

Akin is on Saheed's table. She doesn't want to be separated from him. Why would Funke switch seats with him? Why would Funke want to be at a different table from Saheed? Yemisi's clients in general want to sit next to their spouses, even when they're not in the mood to speak to them. They don't mind being miserable as they eat. After dinner, women will gather together, so will men, separately.

She usually avoids getting involved in planning her clients' seating arrangements because of the sheer drudgery of considering the relationships between people at any given table in Lagos, their alliances, rivalries and politics. She finds her way to Funke's table, which is nearest to the dance floor. Funke has probably done the best she can with her last-minute seating arrangements, but on Saheed's table, Funke has Saheed's business partner, Mustapha, next to the pastor who blames emirs like Mustapha's father for Boko Haram attacks. If Mustapha's father had his way, Nigeria would be an Islamic country. He lobbied for the right to adopt sharia law in Northern Nigeria. Mustapha prefers to play polo there. He founded the first polo-cum-country club in his home state.

Saheed, a one-leg-in-one-leg-out Muslim, courted his friendship for years, inviting him to the polo club in Lagos whenever he was in town. The club veterans made fun of Saheed behind his back. He had only just started taking riding lessons. He barely knew how to mount a horse. They said he would never succeed in aligning himself with a northern aristocrat like Mustapha. But he did. He and Mustapha teamed up to invest in an Islamic banking scheme. How they separated Islam from banking, God only knew.

On the elders' table, Funke has her father, Professor Akande, a hardcore Yoruba secessionist who believes the South West of Nigeria would be better off as a country in its own right, next to a chief who sits on the board of Saheed's company. The chief is from the South South region of Nigeria and is too financially shrewd to be a secessionist. He understands what secessionists don't: that it makes more sense to do business with Nigerians from ethnic groups he can't stand than to demand the partitioning of Nigeria. Still, as an elder statesman of the South South, he attends meetings in his home state to discuss how Nigeria's oil, which is drilled there and has polluted the land, doesn't benefit his people. He assures his people that any concerns they have will be fully addressed whenever the president decides to convene a national conference.

Yemisi remembers her father saying rich Nigerians had no ethnic or religious divisions, but they created them so poor Nigerians could kill each other off. She has had moments of panic at parties in Lagos, imagining a suicide bomber gatecrashing, followed by a violent aftermath with food and blood splattered everywhere, followed by a thought that terrifies her so much she immediately suppresses it—*One bomb at a party like this and half of Nigeria's problems will disappear.*

Unsuitable Ties

She finds her seating card on the table. She is next to Funke and Biola. She is beginning to think Funke switched seats so their husbands can discuss business without interference. She and Funke are the only wives separated from their husbands on the table. Oyinda and Oliver are together across from them. Akin is right next to Saheed on Saheed's table. She imagines herself running over there and yelling, "What is wrong with you? How could you even consider doing business with him at a time like this? Have you no shame?"

The menu distracts her for a while. The first course is salad with goat's cheese or lobster bisque. She goes for the bisque, which turns out to be bland. The main meal is chicken breast in a béchamel-based sauce with steamed vegetables. Her clients are usually not keen on white meat, or any meat mixed with dairy. They don't appreciate al dente vegetables. Or vegetarian meals. The vegetarian meal is a risotto. Oliver is the only one who has requested it.

She is not a food or wine connoisseur, or a conversationalist. Her favorite way to pass time at dinner parties is to listen to other people talking. She avoids looking at them to decode their conversations. Her father taught her how to; he fancied himself an expert on espionage.

"That country is useless. Useless, I tell you."

Biola complaining to Funke about mobile-phone services in Nigeria. Yemisi has heard Nigerians call Nigeria a useless country for more trivial problems: a bad pedicure, a shirt button lost at the dry cleaner's. She calls Nigeria a useless country whenever she gets stuck in traffic.

"They don't practice medicine there. They practice business. Any doctor who wants to practice medicine has left the country and the newly qualified ones are just badly trained."

A man telling Oyinda why she is better off practicing pediatrics in England. His mother was misdiagnosed with malaria in Nigeria, when she had pancreatitis. He is managing director of a cable-television company. Yemisi holds him personally responsible for the latest trend of theme parties in Lagos. Because of E! Entertainment Television and other such networks, her clients want menus to match their themes. They ask for cupcakes and cake pops.

For a moment, she panics over her parents. She must call them in the morning to find out if her mother has had her blood pressure tested, and if her father has seen a doctor about his lower-back pain.

"She carries herself well. She dresses conservatively. What I like most about her is that she is not trying to upstage her husband. She came into that family knowing her place."

Funke talking about Prince William and Kate and making them sound awfully Nigerian.

What is it with clothes? Yemisi thinks. What is it with Nigerians and clothes? It's not as if there is a designer in Paris looking at his collection and saying, "C'est parfait pour mes clientes Nigériennes!"

"I still don't understand the fuss about Pippa."

Biola, doing what she does best.

"Of course I'm against free education!"

The same man who said newly qualified Nigerian doctors were badly trained.

"How can anyone be against free education?"

Oyinda, who laughs even though she's outraged.

"Don't mind him. He's talking rubbish."

The man's wife. Her bluntness is unusual. She may be upset with him over an unrelated matter. She is an interior decorator—a real one, not just an attractive woman who has an eye for color and knows how to put a room together. These days, in Lagos, any woman who can put a meal together can call herself a caterer.

"Free education ruined the school system in Lagos. We used to have good schools before they opened them up to the masses. I went to Saint Greg's. People like us can't send our sons to Saint Greg's anymore."

The man, ignoring his wife.

"I suppose that's one way of looking at it."

Oyinda, disagreeing.

"Don't mind him. He doesn't know what he's talking about."

His wife, refusing to be ignored.

"Did anyone read that article about the Lagos elite?"

Oyinda.

"What article?"

Funke.

"Saheed was mentioned."

Oyinda, soliciting gossip.

"Not that article again."

Funke, pretending to be embarrassed.

"They were just upper-middle-class Nigerians. You can't compare them to the global elite."

Biola, an authority on class since her early schooling in Switzerland.

"It made us look bad to the rest of the world, though. We don't all live lavishly."

Oyinda, who still doesn't realize she is not part of the one percent in Lagos.

"Anyone can live lavishly in Nigeria if they have money. That doesn't mean they have class."

Biola, taking a jab.

"Some elite Nigerians do."

Funke, blocking.

Elite at what? Yemisi thinks. Shopping? What does class mean in Nigeria anyway? Nigerians call themselves upper middle class if they manage to buy a house on a mortgage. Akin once called her high class because she made spaghetti alla puttanesca. English classes cause confusion. American percents are better suited to Nigeria. Besides, who in the world would take seriously an article about people who are of no consequence to anyone but themselves?

"It was shocking to me, actually."

Oliver.

"Really? Why?"

Biola, attempting to bully him.

"That people can be so excessive in the midst of so much poverty."

Oliver, with First World indignation.

"There's poverty in Europe. That's why half of Europe is here."

Biola, with Third World defensiveness.

"Not the kind of poverty you have in Africa, surely."

Oliver, laughing cautiously.

"You look like a world traveler. Which African countries have you been to?"

Biola, condescendingly.

"Oyinda and I went on holiday to Kenya. We hiked up Kilimanjaro for charity."

Oliver, humbly.

"He took photos."

Funke, bored with the conversation. She is an intelligent woman. She may not be as intelligent as Biola, but she practiced law for many years, which was more than Biola did. Biola had a one-year stint at her uncle's firm, then she worked for her father, which amounted to attending boardroom meetings on his behalf. The problem with Funke was that as soon as Saheed made money, she had new concerns. She got involved with a group of women who had similar concerns. Now, if a conversation isn't about their concerns, she is not interested. Biola has to stay on top of issues outside their circle to run her foundation.

"Kenya is very different from Nigeria, economically."

Biola, professorially.

"Yes, I know Nigeria is oil rich, but there is that gap between the rich and the poor, isn't there?"

Oliver, earnestly.

"There is, there is."

Oyinda, who sounds as if she's rocking back and forth.

Yemisi has heard Nigerians refer to themselves as poor because they can't afford to send their children to schools abroad. She would say her house help and catering staff are poor. If they stopped working for a month they might starve, unless they were prepared to beg. Yet they might say beggars on the streets are poor. She gives leftover food to her catering staff after jobs. She pays her house help's hospital bills. Akin thinks they take advantage of her. "They're always sick," he once said. He is polite to them because he is a polite person, but he doesn't trust them. He has the usual anxieties about theft and that other unspoken fear, that no matter how well he treats them, come a revolution, they would turn around and slit his throat.

"I imagine that affluent Nigerians are sufficiently well placed to do something about the economic divide."

Oliver, who doesn't know the caliber of Nigerian he is fraternizing with. He thinks he can shift their consciences. He cannot. He thinks they're capitalists. Poor Nigerians are the capitalists. They have to be. They don't depend on the government for deals; they don't get to dip their hands in state treasuries or commit bank fraud; they don't even get to smell oil money.

"I think every Nigerian should do what they can. I run a foundation. I'm an advocate for the eradication of poverty in Nigeria. I've been invited to the UN to give a talk. It may not be as arduous as a trek up Kilimanjaro, but it's a start."

Biola.

Knockout, Yemisi thinks.

The dessert options are chocolate gateau or tiramisu. She goes for the gateau, which has a glutinous filling that sticks to the roof of her mouth.

After dinner, Funke's mother stands up to lead the room in a prayer. A dignified woman in a vintage aṣọ-oke outfit with matching stole and head tie, she seems unlikely to tolerate extravagance. "Lord," she says, "we ask that You grant Funke wisdom and humility with age."

Saheed makes the toast between pauses, as guests respond to him.

"She is the love of my life."

"Ah!"

"I am forever indebted to her."

"Ah!"

"And to my in-laws, Professor and Mrs. Akande."

Where are his parents? Yemisi thinks. He flies everyone else around the globe. Why couldn't he fly them here? All she's ever heard about Saheed's parents is that they live in their hometown.

The guests stand up to clink glasses. They sing "For She's a Jolly Good Fellow" and sit down.

"Well," Oyinda says afterward. "That was more like an anniversary toast. You know, I'd much prefer to celebrate my twenty-fifth wedding anniversary than my fiftieth birthday."

Oyinda knows full well that given a choice, Nigerian women will celebrate their birthdays before any wedding anniversary.

"It's envy," Biola says, out of nowhere. "It's all envy at the end of the day."

"Yes," Funke murmurs. "It is."

Yemisi can't decide if they are talking about Oyinda or Oliver. Then she guesses from Funke's sober expression that Biola may have been referring to someone else. She reconsiders a rumor, which she initially ignored, that Saheed has several girlfriends in Lagos he supports financially, including one who has a son by him. That could explain why Funke is not sitting with him.

The DJ, who has been setting up his equipment on the dance floor, begins to play Afropop. Oyinda and Oliver get up to dance, followed by Funke and Biola and other couples on their table. Women take over the dance floor. Akin won't dance in public. He thinks it emasculates him. Yemisi, a self-confessed lousy dancer, stays in her chair and watches. Oyinda and Oliver do a calypso dance as Funke and Biola point at each other and sing, "I'm hot and you're not," to a D'banj song.

The men on Saheed's table finally disperse and head for the dance floor to join their wives. Only then does Akin remember her. He smiles as he approaches her, sits in the chair next to hers and then frowns.

"What's wrong?" he asks.

"Nothing," she says.

"Sure?"

"Sure."

"Having a good time?"

"Yeah."

He rubs her knee. They watch other couples on the dance floor. Funke is dancing with Saheed, side by side rather than face to face.

"What were you and Saheed talking about?"

"He wanted my advice."

"On?"

"Some business idea."

"I knew it! That's why they separated us!"

"Who separated us? Why?"

She softens her voice. He might retreat back to Saheed's table.

"What business idea?"

"He wants to invest in a country club."

"Where?"

"Somewhere off Lekki Expressway, past our estate. Mustapha is involved."

"Are you involved?"

"You think I'm stupid?"

"It's not about being stupid."

"What is it about?"

What is it about? she thinks. Saheed has not been charged. The EFCC may never even charge him. This is his chance to play country clubs with Mustapha.

"Are you sure you're all right?" Akin asks, narrowing his eyes.

"Why do you keep asking?"

"I mean, I thought it worked out well that we were on separate tables. You said you wanted to stay as far away as possible."

"I know, I know."

She has also said he shouldn't take her literally.

He laughs. "Or are we still on the matter of my choice of tie?"

She smiles. "Of course not."

DEBT

The lighting in the department store reminds her of hospitals. She walks through the entrance ignoring the display, a Plexiglas table on top of which are vases in shades of orange, yellow and green. On both sides of the table are white mannequins in floral summer dresses. She barely pays attention to them, either. She is thinking of her mom. In particular, of how she waited in hospital corridors for her to come out of maternity wards when she was a girl. Her mom, who still works as a nurse in New Jersey, lives in an apartment in Hackensack, about twenty minutes away by car. She has driven from Pennsylvania to see her mom at home today, and is dreading the visit, which is partly why she has stopped at this mall on Route 4. She also hopes to find a handbag she has been looking for.

She heads for the general handbag section. She has never been interested in bags with logos, "the Cs, Gs, Fs and LVs," as she calls them. Their departments are almost identically ordered.

Their bags are in compartments on back walls, and the wallets and other accessories are in display cases farther up front. One department has a gray carpet; another, laminated flooring that resembles black and white tiles. Louis Vuitton has what looks like hardwood flooring, with a vintage malle cabine across from the register.

The assistant in the general handbag section is a blonde with a well-rehearsed smile.

"Can I help you?"

"I think so."

She points at a black, leather tote bag with a crisscross weave.

The assistant widens her eyes. "Oh, I love that bag! I wish I could afford to buy it."

"Me, too," she says.

Another assistant may not have been as candid, or may even have ignored her. With her skinny jeans, cropped T-shirt and hair weave, she could be any twentysomething black woman. There is no way of telling that she works for a Big Four accountancy firm as a consultant and provides advisory services to Fortune 500 companies. Or that she earns a six-figure salary, even as her credit score has recently dropped because she has maxed out all her cards. Her first name, Grace, grants her a generic black pass as well, but not her Yoruba last name, Oladimeji.

The assistant strokes the bag before handing it to Grace. Grace cradles it and runs her hand over the weave patterns. The texture of the bag tingles her fingers, and the smell of new leather gives her a sensation similar to a head rush.

"It's beautiful," the assistant says.

"It is," Grace says.

Debt

"It will stay with you forever."

"It will."

"Would you like me to wrap it up for you?"

Grace clutches the bag. "Please give me a moment to think about this."

The assistant flops her wrist. "Oh, take your time, honey. You have plenty of time. Walk around for as long as you want and I'll be here. I'm not going anywhere soon and it's all right to have second thoughts. Buying a bag like this is a lifetime commitment."

Grace hands the bag back to the assistant who perhaps meant to say investment instead of commitment. She could invest the money she is about to spend on the bag, but she can't be committed to one bag when she has others. Besides, she will soon see another, obsess over it and might even travel this far to find it.

"Thanks," she says to the assistant. "It won't take me long."

She would like to think she and the assistant have had a genuine connection. She would even want to believe the assistant would be partial to her if another shopper comes along and wants to buy the same bag. She panics as she walks away, hoping it will still be available when she returns.

She prefers to shop online. Shopping online gives her some degree of anonymity and control. She can also return an item she is not satisfied with simply by filling out a form and arranging a UPS pickup. But she uses her debit card to shop now, which might be a problem if she goes back to the convenience of shopping online. She can't help herself. She will only further ruin her credit.

She heads for the shoe section and ends up at the sales racks, where she chooses a pair of black-and-white-striped

Italian-made flats. She crouches as she struggles to put them on and nearly tumbles over when an assistant in a tight-fitting black suit approaches her, his dreadlocks pulled back in a bun.

"Are you okay there?" he asks.

"Yes," she says, sounding breathless as she straightens up.

"You could sit, you know."

She smiles apologetically. "I know."

He studies her feet. "They look kind of snug to me. You might want to go a half size up."

"They're my size, actually."

"The fit is narrow."

"I'm all right with that."

He lifts his forefinger. "Well, if they're comfortable on."

She pulls off the shoes by their heels as he walks away. For a moment she considers leaving them on the floor in retaliation, but she picks them up and returns them to the rack. She has worked as an assistant in a shoe store before and would get mad whenever customers left shoes they'd tried on lying around.

She was born in Nigeria. She and her mom immigrated to America when she was two years old. According to her mom, they left Nigeria because her father became a polygamist after he received a chieftaincy title. He married a second wife who had a son by him, and from then on neglected Grace and her mom, even though he could afford to take care of both families.

The idea of having a chief for a father was too remote for Grace to grasp when she was a girl, having never been back to Nigeria. Her mom had no photos of him, but once in a while would look at Grace's widow's peak and say, "You look just like him." Grace had watched *Coming to America*, her only frame of reference for the customs of African royalty. She imagined her father dressed like Arsenio Hall in the movie, in a suit and a Karakul cap. Her mom referred to him as a businessman, which at first surprised her because she had thought his job was to be part of a king's entourage. When she was old enough to ask for details, she found out he imported electronic goods from England and sold them in Nigeria. He owned a storied shopping plaza in Lagos, and his electronics store took up the entire ground floor.

Grace and her mom had lived in Teaneck before they moved to Hackensack. She doesn't remember their apartment in Teaneck. She went to day care there while her mom worked in retail and studied for her nursing exams. She attended elementary school in Hackensack when her mom started working as a nurse. Once her mom bought a car, they would drive to the mall every weekend. She hated the mall back then. She would get bored waiting for her mom to browse stores, but she enjoyed the cinnamon buns and lemonade her mom bought her at the food court. She loved the lights in the mall at Christmastime, especially. Apparently, she was scared of Father Christmas, as her mom calls Santa Claus, but she doesn't remember that.

She didn't care for the mall until she was in middle school, where she was teased for being a nerd and having nappy hair. She would eagerly go to the mall with her mom, who would give her enough money to buy cheap, shiny trinkets. Her mom bought her her first music CD, *The Miseducation of Lauryn Hill*, at the mall and they would sing along to it in the car. She started going to the mall on her own when she left middle school for a Catholic high school in Paramus. Sometimes she met her best friend, Ashley, there. Ashley's parents were from the Philippines and they owned a family grocery store. She and Ashley had a play rivalry over which moms were pushier, Asian or African moms. She was one of a few girls in school who were not dating. Her mom, as if to encourage her to stay that way, would give her money to buy makeup, perfume, jeans, T-shirts, anything she wanted from the mall.

There was a time in middle school when Grace was of the impression that shopping on weekends was the American way of life and all she needed to aspire to. In high school, she became cynical about shopping. She bought Kanye West's *The College Dropout* and listened to "All Falls Down" over and over, as if the lyrics were written for her: she was a single black female and she was addicted to retail. But the mall, for her, was more an escape from home now. She knew her mom took Prozac because of the stress of work. She could cope with her mom taking Prozac until her mom began to take Xanax as well.

She walks through the perfumery section, passing Hermès, Ferragamo and Marc Jacobs perfumes on glass shelves. She wears Marc Jacobs' Daisy. She has never stopped to try Jo Malone of London perfumes, but the bottles always grab her attention. There is a display of samples labeled Citrus, Fruity, Light Floral, Floral and Woody. The perfumes range from clear to yellowy tones. A brunette assistant in a leopard-print dress and coral lipstick holds up a bottle of some other perfume, but Grace shakes her head and passes her.

The cosmetics section resembles a collection of giant artist palettes. Bobbi Brown has a few customers, MAC has more than a few. Chanel has a whole department, which is empty but for a middle-aged woman in a white linen pantsuit, and an assistant dressed in black. Kiehl's has a skeleton in a bow tie and a doctor's coat. Grace stops to try a hand lotion as she reconsiders buying the bag. She really doesn't need another bag, but having this one would say of her that she is stylish rather than fashion conscious. That she is confident enough not to care about making a fashion statement.

Her reasoning amuses her. How pathetic is that? she thinks, rubbing her hands together until the lotion is absorbed.

Her mom initially mixed with other Nigerians in America, but ended up falling out with them. The women were gossipy and competitive, she said, and the men would use and abuse women, if they could. Grace didn't meet many Nigerians her own age until she went to college. Most of them were American-born children of immigrants, a handful of whom had attended private schools because their parents were in law, medicine and other such professions. To her, the private school kids were privileged and bound to end up in an Ivy League college, but they complained about not being eligible for financial aid, as she was. She also met Nigerians from Nigeria, who had been educated partly there and partly in English boarding schools, or "public schools," as they called them. They had been all over Europe. They traveled to London in the summer and to Lagos for Christmas. They planned to return to Nigeria after they graduated.

One of them asked why her name was Grace. She asked why he wanted to know. He said his housegirl in Nigeria was called Grace, and only housegirls had names like Grace, Mercy, Patience, Comfort and Joy. "I am Catholic," she said. She ignored him after that, but she made friends with other Nigeria-Nigerians who were on her business program. They were called Tara, Lali, Kit and Zak. Their names had been shortened: Tara was Omotara, a Yoruba name. Lali was Alali, a Kalabari name.

Kit was Akitoye. He, too, was Yoruba. Zak was Zakaria. He was Hausa, but his name was Arabic. She would have dinner with Tara and Lali now and then, but when she suggested they all go to a Senegalese restaurant for dinner on Nigeria's Independence Day for an African night out, Kit said that was un-Nigerian. "We don't do the motherland thing there," he said. "You lot here are setting us back."

She warmed to them because she was a Britophile. She read British literature and watched British movies. Kit was like a Nigerian Oscar Wilde because he had that cutting-wit persona going for him. Tara's posh English accent reminded her of Agatha Runcible's in the movie *Bright Young Things*, though Tara denied it. They all walked around as if they belonged wherever they went. She wasn't ashamed of being Nigerian, but she wished she had their worldliness and unconscious pride. During Thanksgiving break, she asked her mom, "How come you didn't tell me about Nigerians like them?" Her mom sniffed, as if they were beneath her. "I never mixed with Nigerians like them."

She takes the escalator to the second floor and looks down on the fine-jewelry section. She has a pair of diamond stud earrings, but other than that she doesn't wear jewelry. Her mom used to buy gold jewelry, earrings, necklaces and bracelets, though her mom often said 14-karat gold was American and Nigerians preferred 18-karat gold.

Upstairs she passes a male assistant with spiked hair talking to a teenage girl with a purple rinse.

"Your hair color will go with anything," the assistant says.

"Yeah," the girl says.

"Look at it this way," the assistant says, with a laugh. "It has to."

"Yeah," the girl says, smoothing her hair back.

Debt

Grace thinks about the assistant in the handbag section who had won her over the same way. Their selling method is like indoctrination. She has recently been paid, so she has enough money for the bag, but she won't have much to spend after she's paid her rent, car lease, credit card bills and other expenses. She definitely won't be able to eat out this month if she buys the bag, and eating out is all she ever does to socialize these days. Spending nights at home watching television would be miserable. She wishes she had a dog. She has always wanted a dog. A small, cute dog like a Lhasa Apso or a Yorkie. But at the same time she's glad she's never had one. She can't imagine having to give a dog away because she is in a financial mess.

When she was in college, she was sometimes too broke to go out with Tara and Lali. They would eat at restaurants she couldn't afford to eat at. She did odd retail jobs on the weekends to make extra money. Tara and Lali didn't work. They didn't have to, and they had visa restrictions. Her jobs gave her reasons to turn down their invitations, but whenever she had enough money, she would go out with them. All she'd ever heard about Nigeria on the news was that it was a country with email scammers and corrupt leaders. By her mom's account, Lagos was the same filthy, congested city it was when they left, and if they returned, they would be robbed of their belongings and blown up by Boko Haram.

Tara and Lali just talked about the Nigerian social scenes in Lagos and London. In London, there were Nigerian hangouts. She found it weird when they referred to Nigerian students there as rich kids. Perhaps those students were children of billionaires. Tara's last boyfriend was one. His mother was an oil dealer. He was sweet in private, Tara said, but she broke up with him because he was embarrassing in public. He would reserve tables in clubs and order champagne like some hard hip-hop mogul when he was just a spoiled brat who had never taken public transportation. In Lagos, there were one or two clubs, but they went out of fashion pretty quickly, so friends got together, hired halls and Afropop MCs and sold tickets. Afropop was huge in Lagos, but once in a while American hip-hop MCs and R&B singers flew in for concerts. Chris Brown and Rick Ross had recently been there.

Of course, she, Tara and Lali talked about guys. She learned that Nigerians like them didn't have random hookups because they had to be careful about their reputations. Everyone knew everyone and parents talked. They asked what sort of guy she was into and she said, "He would have to be black and he would have to be smart. Sorry, but I can't deal with a dumb pretty boy." Lali asked, "Why does he have to be black?" Lali had an angular face with a permanently inquiring expression. "I don't look at other races that way," Grace said. "Why not?" Lali asked. "I just don't," Grace said, and shrugged.

Lali was always involved in organizing panels on student diversity and student rights, perhaps because she'd had some schooling in America. She went to a boarding school in England called Wycombe Abbey, but her parents, who had attended college in America, wanted her to get into the American system of education sooner, so she left Wycombe Abbey for Exeter.

Tara had only dated Nigerians, but she had all these standards they had to meet. They had to be well-educated and well-spoken. They couldn't be too Nigerian. She couldn't take too Nigerian. Tara had dated Yoruba guys, mostly. She did not date other Africans. She would definitely not date an African American or a West Indian. "They would probably not want to date you because you're African," Lali said. Tara's accent immediately turned Nigerian. "And so?"

Tara had dimples and one of those likeable faces that, no matter what came out of her mouth, you forgave her. She kept saying, "And so?" as Lali repeatedly called her stuck-up. Grace laughed so hard she was in tears. She had never met anyone as unapologetically prejudiced as Tara. Lali would date anyone. She had a thing for Chinese guys with tans.

With Kit and Zak, Grace became their go-to person for insights African American. They both thought Americans were overly preoccupied with racial issues. Kit said racism was clearly a sign of stupidity so it ought to be ignored. Zak couldn't understand the fuss about the N-word because it was used freely in rap. They refused to listen to any talk about charity in Africa, though. Once, when she brought up a charitable cause relating to Africa, Kit called charity a racket and Zak said he was sick of celebrities using Africa to improve their image. Kit could be arrogant, and Zak was a bit on the quiet side. They were both into European girls. They didn't think that was a big deal. Grace didn't either. She didn't want them, so anyone could have them, but she did wonder why, if they were so international, they only went for European girls.

She reaches the casuals section on the second floor and admires the view as if it is an architectural design. There are rails of black and white clothing, rails of clothing in muted colors like beige and gray, and others with striking colors she guesses are called citrus yellow and peacock green. Why is she ashamed of shopping? Why does she see shopping as a senseless activity? The signs for Splendid and Theory labels remind her of poetry and philosophy.

The perfume and cosmetics sections downstairs reminded her of chemistry and art, and the Louis Vuitton department of language and history, when she saw the vintage malle cabine.

I'm so fucked, she thinks.

In college, she met a guy called Peter who was in his second year of engineering. Peter's parents were pharmacists, and they were from Nigeria. They were Bendelites. He explained that meant they were from somewhere in the midwest of Nigeria. They had immigrated to America in the 1980s, and Peter was born and raised in Mississippi. His family was messed up, more messed up than hers, so messed up she could tell him about her mom taking pills. His parents were strict Catholics and Republican. They voted for George Bush, supported the war in Iraq and were convinced President Obama was Muslim.

She was too scared to ask if they were birthers, but from what Peter told her about them, they were the sort of African immigrants who considered it a privilege to be seen as good blacks. To her, they were patronized. Peter must have thought so as well because he rebelled against them. He'd played baseball in high school until he got too friendly with some blue-eyed cheerleader whose dad found out. The man threatened to shoot him. Instead of reporting the man to the police, Peter's parents asked if Peter had fornicated with his daughter. "I mean," Peter said, "what happened to thou shalt not kill?"

His parents never reported the incident because the man worked for the mayor's office. They hoped Peter would stay out of trouble for the rest of high school and get a baseball scholarship to help with his college fees. Instead, Peter stopped playing baseball and started wearing "thug-like apparel," as his dad said, "and speaking in a ghetto-like manner." His parents were worried he was taking drugs. Peter didn't do drugs; he also studied hard. He felt he owed his parents for paying his tuition. He was determined to pay them back as soon as he could. He was resentful of Tara and others, who could take their parents' support for granted. He called them the native bourgeoisie. He had read Fanon's *The Wretched of the Earth*. "I thought you were bougie," he said. "They're like bougie beyond belief."

He would deliberately interrupt Kit and Zak when they were talking and say, "Wait, what?" as if he couldn't understand them. They, in turn, would exaggerate their English accents to suggest he was parochial. Grace didn't always understand the English slang Tara and Lali used, like "plonker" and "prat," but it wasn't that hard to figure out what they meant: Zak was a plonker and Kit was a prat. Peter didn't believe they were into girls at all because of the pastel-colored Oxford shirts they wore, even though she argued they looked no different from preppy African American students. "Yeah, whatever," he'd say. "They gay."

Peter was the first guy she hooked up with in college, and they continued to hook up now and then until he graduated and moved to Texas to work for an oil company. But he was too much of a jock for her. He had to be on the winning team. She would be lying in bed with him, telling him she was feeling low, and he would tell her to get up and go for a run. He called her hardheaded whenever they argued. She called him stupid. After college, they messaged each other on Facebook a few times, but she eventually thought there was no point. He got married early anyway, to a woman named Monique. Her parents were from Haiti, and she was a CPA. She had a self-assured and capable look about her. She was a Michelle Obama fan, but okay with his parents' views. She was Catholic as well, which was perfect.

Grace got an invitation to their wedding, but she didn't go because she thought it would be awkward.

She notices a uniformed security guard with a badge watching her. He might just be making the usual tribal eye contact. There are other black shoppers in the casuals section: a woman with long gray braids and a man in a Hawaiian shirt and a Panama hat. She has been watched and followed in stores before, but she has never been stopped. Even if she were, she would still shop. Only when pressured by overenthusiastic assistants does she feel inclined to walk out of stores.

She ought to get the bag instead of wandering around, she thinks. She makes a show of looking for the down escalator in case the security guard is suspicious of her.

The more Xanax her mom took, the more Grace came to the mall. The first time she maxed out a credit card she bought a leather jacket. Her mom was careful with money, even while taking her pills. She and her mom did not have the same sense of style. She went for simple and understated; her mom preferred embroidery and other embellishments. She never tried to advise her mom on clothes, but her mom found her taste expensive. Her mom was a hoarder. She was not. She gave away what she no longer used to charity.

She still does, but has become manic about making sure her wardrobe remains trim. Every year, she donates clothes. Every month, she keeps up with her credit card minimum payments because she is paranoid that debt collectors will call her at work. She can't tell anyone about her bills. Not her mom or her work colleagues, who would probably think she is dumb to get into so much debt.

Debt

She once overheard a client talking about an article on how much basketball players spent. "It's low self-esteem," he said. "If you think about it, who spends the most on clothes and bling? Women and—uh—see what I'm saying?" What offended her most was his use of the word "bling."

She reaches the ground floor, her heart rate increasing as she heads for the handbag section. She doesn't see the bag when she gets there. She doesn't see the assistant, either.

"There you are!" the assistant says, behind her, causing her to jump.

She pats her chest. "Is it . . . still available?"

"Of course it is. I put it aside for you."

"You did that for me?"

"I saw how much you wanted it. I've seen that look before. Here."

The assistant retrieves the bag from behind the counter. The bag seems to have shrunk and it could be a two-hundred-dollar bag now. Why does she want it so badly?

"I'm addicted to shopping," she cries out.

The assistant laughs. "Oh, honey, we all are."

Grace hands over her driver's license and debit card after the assistant wraps the bag carefully in tissue. Her card is unlikely to be declined, but she is nervous anyway.

"I'm not even going to try and pronounce your last name," the assistant murmurs.

She drives to her mom's apartment thinking about her father. She has never thought of him as her dad. Her mom once told her his other wife had used juju to lure him and would use juju to stop anyone from getting close to him. She was still curious enough to want to contact him. She tried to Google him, but her hands trembled so much she kept misspelling Oladimeji, then she couldn't hit Enter. Her heart pounded so loudly she thought her ears might pop. She was sure that if she saw an article on him or a photograph of him, she would pass out.

She has given up on the idea of contacting her father. He will probably turn out to be as uncaring as her mom said he was, and deny or reject her. She doesn't want to be one of those women who, having been abandoned by their fathers, follow the rest of the script, forever searching for substitutes in other men. She has no time for nonsense when it comes to men. Any type of bad behavior and it's, "Buh-bye."

Her ex-boyfriend, Courtney, a Jamaican financial planner who had a knack for coming up with platitudes at the wrong times, with a lilt and pauses in between, said she was scared of committing to relationships because she was broken. She was broken inside. She was broken inside because of her father. Because of her father, she was unable to make herself vulnerable. Vulnerable to other men. Courtney would sulk as if she had deprived him of his right to hurt her. As far as she was concerned, Courtney just couldn't accept the fact that she was as uncommitted as he was, so he dumped her.

She parks her car on the street adjacent to her mom's. The last time she was here, her mom accused her of not visiting enough. She walks to her mom's block wondering what kind of mood she will find her in today. Her mom's metallic-gray Honda CR-V is on the street, which means the parking lot behind the block must be full. She steps on a pavement crack she religiously avoided when she lived there.

Her mom's neighbor, Mrs. Murphy, a widow who gave her a ladybug pin for good luck when she was a girl, and who has since

Debt

moved to Florida, would say to her, "Step on a crack, break your mother's back." In college, she found out the original saying was, "Step on a crack, turn your mother black."

She presses the buzzer. When her mom answers, she says, "It's me," and walks up the stairs remembering when she was brave enough to jump down each flight.

"I called you," her mom says, opening the door.

"When?"

"Just now. I even called you at home. Several times."

"You did?"

Grace checks her cell phone. Her mom is in baby-blue velour sweatpants and a matching T-shirt with crystal studs. At home, her mom wears a black silk scarf to preserve her hairstyles. She wishes she had thick hair like her mom's. Hers is thinning around her temples because of her hair weaves.

She has a few missed calls. "Hey, you did call!"

"Why didn't you answer?"

"I was driving."

She wants to confess that she was at the mall. She would like to tell her mom she has a shopping habit, and blame it on her, but that wouldn't be true, or fair. Her mom has evidence of past shopping escapades all over her apartment. In her bedroom, there are bags full of clothes with tags. In her kitchen, there are opened boxes of unused electrical appliances: a food processor, a robotic vacuum cleaner. In her bathroom are tubs of creams and bath salts. Her mom rarely buys clothes anymore, especially if they're made in China.

"I'm going back to Nigeria," her mom says, lying on the sofa in the living room.

"What happened?" she asks.

She doesn't ask why. She's heard this before. Something happens at work or elsewhere, and her mom says she is going back to Nigeria for good, even though she can't afford to. She does a good job of hiding her pill habit at work, but at home she is lethargic and negative.

"I'm tired of this country," her mom says. "They work you too hard and they're too racist."

Grace sits in a chair. "You've always known that."

"I'm getting older."

"I won't be able to visit you in Nigeria."

"God forbid I die in America. I beg you, whatever you do, don't bury me here."

"Mom, you're too young to talk like this."

She can't bear her mom talking about death. She can't bear her mom talking to her about men, either. Recently, her mom has been nagging her about finding a nice Nigerian man in America. She doesn't let her mom finish her sentences. "Mom," she says, over and over, getting louder until her mom says, "Okay, I'm just telling you."

She was in her final year of high school and suffering from senioritis when her mom started taking Xanax. She had already been admitted to college via an Early Decision application. All she wanted to do was go out with her friends and go on a date for once. A really cute guy in school called Demetrius asked her out to a movie. He played soccer and so badly wanted to get into Rutgers University. "Is he Greek or what?" her mom asked. "He's African American," Grace said. "These people and their funny names," her mom said. "What people? What funny names?" Grace asked. "What do his parents do anyway?" her mom asked. Demetrius' mom was a nurse and they weren't in contact with

Debt

his dad. "I don't like single parent setups," her mom said. "What are we?" Grace asked.

Her mom went down her usual checklist of the dangers of teen life in America: sex, drugs, alcohol. "Stick to Americans like Ashley," her mom said. "Mom, you don't know Ashley," Grace said.

Ashley drank and smoked weed. She was going out with a guy called Luis her parents couldn't stand. She would tell them she was meeting Grace at the mall and meet Luis there. Grace didn't say any of this, but she argued with her mom until she was granted permission to go on the date with Demetrius.

Demetrius was the first guy she made out with. She never watched the movie. She pulled an Ashley on her mom from then on and spent time with him at the mall until she went to college. She cried when they broke up—actually, she cried because he cried, but their breakup was still traumatic. But before that, she noticed her mom was sleeping longer than usual and becoming increasingly irritable. She would ask, "Why are you yelling?" or "What are you yelling for?" Her mom would tell her to shut up or threaten to slap her. She could not mention the pills; instead, she Googled them to check that they didn't interact and researched their side effects. She would sleep with her bedroom door open so she could hear her mom breathing. One day, when her mom started whining about America again, she asked her, "Why did you come here, then?" Her mom said, "I did it for you." Grace said, "I was only two. I had no say." Her mom said, "Look at you. You're not even grateful."

Today, her mom tells her why she is tired of America. One night, the hospital called her in to serve as a translator when a Nigerian woman showed up at the emergency room in labor.

"The foolish woman claimed she couldn't speak English. She said she could only speak Yoruba so they called me in, in my free time. She had no record of prenatal care. No record whatsoever in America, and she was telling me her records were in Nigeria. She had prenatal care there. Worse, she was having twins. So she put her life and her children's lives at risk so they would be born in America. She had no insurance and no intention of paying her bills. Hah! Nigerians!"

"We're special," Grace says.

"Actually," her mom says, "I can never go back to that country."

Grace laughs. "Mom, will you make up your mind?"

It is a good visit. Or at least, she leaves in an okay mood. Perhaps she timed her entrance and exit perfectly this time. If she left too early, her mom would have been pissed. If she left too late, she would be pissed.

Her mom had already had lunch, but Grace ate some of her chicken stew with rice and fried plantains. When she was younger, she couldn't understand why her mom wouldn't just go to Pathmark to buy her ingredients. Instead, she chose to go all the way to Paterson to get fresh chicken, habaneros and ripe plantains, as if they lived somewhere in Nigeria. Now, she knows why. She has never been able to replicate the taste of her mom's chicken stews.

They almost, almost got into an argument when her mom asked, "How's your friend Ashley?"

Ashley worked for a law firm in New York. She wanted to quit and move back to New Jersey to open a bakery.

Grace said, "Mom, will you please stop asking me about Ashley?"

Debt

"I just want to know. How come you don't see her anymore?"

"We're in touch on Facebook."

"She was such a nice, polite girl. Asians are like Africans, you know. They raise their children well."

Grace said, "I'd better go."

She can't tell how her mom really feels about America. Her mom is in a constant state of contradiction about America and Americans. She suspects her mom is envious of Nigerians in Nigeria. Maybe that was what her mom's reaction to the pregnant woman was about. Not that the woman would not pay her hospital bills, but that she would return to Nigeria with her twins.

She, too, was kind of envious when Tara and the rest returned to Nigeria. Tara was CEO of her own marketing company. Her clients were small and medium enterprises, like recycling companies and employment agencies. They were not cutting-edge start-ups, but they were relevant and profitable. Lali was director of her own non-governmental organization. She was trying to inspire young Nigerians to get more involved in the democratic process. She received a THISDAY award, which Bill Clinton, of all people, presented to her. Zak worked for his uncle, who was the wealthiest man in Nigeria. Or was it Africa? His uncle manufactured cement, anyhow. Kit was with a new telecommunications company. He was always on the move. The last time she heard from him, he was in Saudi Arabia. "What the hell are you doing in Saudi?" she asked. "Trying my best not to get beheaded," Kit said.

She was just beginning to adjust to being a minority in her firm and the only black woman in her department. She got herself a small tattoo below her navel, a stamp saying "Made in

Nigeria." After which, she imagined her tattoo stretching when she had her first child, and shriveling up as she aged.

As she heads back to Philadelphia, she considers returning the bag, but she passes the exit to the mall and keeps driving. The farther she drives, the more difficult it is to turn back, until it is too late to. She glances at her shopping bag on the passenger seat. She knows better, she thinks. Why does she keep doing this? Perhaps she has an addiction gene. She read somewhere that addiction is hereditary. For a while she worries that she's inherited depression.

When she gets home, she puts her shopping bag in her television chair. There are several messages on her phone. She checks her incoming calls. Some are the calls her mom made; others, from numbers she can't identify, must be from the credit card companies that keep calling her to apply for more credit. She presses the Delete button twice and erases them.

HOUSEKEEPING

The hotel sucks. It isn't the one she usually stays in when she is in Atlanta, but that hotel was booked up for Memorial Day weekend. She is too tired to drive around looking for another, so she checks into a suite on the second floor.

The suite has a plaid sofa, framed prints of wooded areas and plastic ferns in baskets. The linoleum floor in the kitchenette is sticky, and the microwave stained with popcorn butter. A calendar on the fridge says that tonight's dinner is baked potatoes and chili. She's already stopped to eat in a Caribbean restaurant at a strip mall on her way. She will be here until Sunday morning, and on Saturday night will go to her cousin Bolaji's party. Bolaji lives in Alpharetta and works as a systems analyst downtown. At work, his colleagues call him "B.J." So does she whenever she teases him because his accent is more American than Nigerian these days. Her own colleagues call her "Abi," which is short for Abiodun. She is still not used to that.

She lifts the mattress to check for bedbugs and disinfects the remote control and bedside phone with Clorox wipes. There is a spot of what looks like ketchup on the receiver, but it could well be blood. She wipes it off, then unpacks her bag before having a shower and changing into striped drawstring pajama pants and a tank top.

As she brushes her teeth for the night, she thinks of her ex, Femi, who lives in New Jersey. Femi was convinced she was obsessive compulsive because of her habit of checking and cleaning hotels before settling in. She ignored his attempts to diagnose her. He was an accountant, not a psychiatrist, she often reminded him.

She is an ER physician and works nights in Pine Springs, Mississippi, where she lives. Normally, she is reluctant to take sleeping aids during the day, as she is afraid of developing a dependency on them. They might also make her drowsy when she's supposed to be awake. But she has driven for over four hours from Pine Springs and is finding it hard to fall asleep, so she takes an Ambien, throws back the flowery bedspread and slips into the sheets.

Lying there, at first she thinks it is her imagination, but she can smell curry. Yes, there is a curry smell coming from the next suite. She calls the front desk to complain.

"Front desk."

"Yes, this is room 218."

"Yes, ma'am."

"I can smell curry in my room. I think it's coming from next door."

"Um, must be a long-stay guest."

"Long stay?"

"Yes. We have a few of them. They're from um, India, taking an IT course."

He is the receptionist who checked her in, a young African American guy with a diamond stud earring.

"Would you like to move to another room?"

"No, that's okay. I just wondered where the smell was coming from."

"It might not get better."

"I'll live. Thanks."

She wrinkles her nose as she hangs up. Perhaps she should have agreed to move, but it is getting late now. Her joints ache, as if she is recovering from a cold: the cumulative effect of not getting enough REM sleep. The digital clock by her bedside tells her it is 8:38 PM. She buries her head under her pillow to lessen the smell of curry.

Tonight, she can't get certain patients out of her mind. There is the redhead girl who overdosed on meth. Her friends brought her to the ER. They claimed they were watching a DVD when she just blacked out. Her heart stopped beating and someone in the ER (who was it, now?) made an inappropriate remark about her Brazilian wax. There is the obese woman who came in bleeding from a stab wound. She was wearing a shower cap and stank of alcohol. It turned out she was diabetic. A nurse was assisting her into a gown when she fell to the floor and dragged the nurse down with her. She lay there howling as the nurse stood up and walked off rubbing her bruised arm. No one could shift that woman. The fire brigade had to come in.

Her most memorable patient was a skinny man with highlights who showed up with half an apple in his rectum.

He claimed he had slipped at Wal-Mart in the produce section when he was wearing shorts. She told her colleagues, Drs. Khan and Fernandez, about him, and Fernandez asked, "Wait, wait, so he wasn't wearing underpants?"

Fernandez makes jokes like that. He once had a patient who was headbutted by a deer. "Wasn't hunting for one neither," the patient said. "But you sure caught one," Fernandez said. The patient had been driving his truck on a winding road when the deer ran out from nowhere. He swerved to avoid it and the deer jumped through his window. "At least he was wearing a seatbelt," Fernandez said.

Most of Abi's patients are teenagers who were not wearing seatbelts. They are brought in after single-car accidents or rollovers in trucks. It pains her to see patients like this, too young, dying for no good reason, but she could well be in Nigeria today, in private practice, and making a reasonable living by doling out unwarranted malaria pills to patients.

Here in America, she makes more money, and she is terrible with hers. She deposits it in a bank. Femi thought that wasn't smart. Of course, he was jealous of her—or rather, of her money. He would have to work years to make as much as she does per annum. Not that she is gloating.

She lifts the pillow from her head so she can breathe freely and remembers that B.J. suggested she buy foreclosed houses in Atlanta and rent them out, as he does. B.J. is good with investing, but he also spends a lot. He throws a party on either Labor Day or Memorial Day. For this one, he's hiring a DJ to play soul oldies and a Nigerian caterer who is popular with the community in Atlanta. He has invited about a hundred guests, and everyone has to show up in jeans and white shirts.

Housekeeping

The year before, he had a highlife party, and the dress code was traditional wear. She was in an ankara up-and-down and Femi was in a navy agbada. He flew in from New Jersey. She remembers Mercedes after Mercedes parked outside B.J.'s house. She finds Nigerians in Atlanta acquisitive, Nigerians in America in general. Professional Nigerians. They have that "We have arrived" mentality: buy, buy, buy.

In Pine Springs, there are other Nigerian doctors, internists and pediatricians mostly. Their wives are enamored with going to the mall. They take their children there because there is nothing much else to do. Once in a while, Fernandez invites her and Khan for a potluck dinner. Fernandez's wife loves to cook. She makes a pork roast with beans, while Khan and his wife bring basmati rice and grilled shrimp. Abi brings fried plantains. Sometimes, Fernandez invites Linda Abernathy, presumably so Abi won't be the only single guest. Linda always shows up with a red velvet cake for dessert. She is a dentist from Meharry Medical College and is paying off her student loans. After dinner, Fernandez makes Cuban coffee, by which time Abi has a tendency to stir up political debates, as Nigerians do.

She once made the mistake of telling Fernandez she would like to visit Cuba and he dismissed that as a terrible idea. "Think about it," he explained. "Why would anyone risk their life to cross the sea on a—excuse my French—Goddamn inner tube if things are so wonderful over there?" To make peace, Abi said Nigerians had been known to hide in the wheel wells of planes flying from Lagos to London. She has learned not to discuss the presidential primaries with Fernandez. The only issues they can agree on are immigration and the cost of gas. Khan is less argumentative and is reticent about politics. It was hard to get him to say much about Bhutto's assassination, except, "Oh, it's very sad." He admits he finds Americans annoyingly intrusive after 9/11, wanting to reach out and understand his culture. He and his wife meet people in Pine Springs who ask if they speak Islamic. "It was better when they were blissfully ignorant," he said.

Their potluck dinners are respite. Linda, who was born in Tuscaloosa, doesn't feel as if she belongs in Pine Springs either. The first time they met, Linda had asked, "So what is an African doctor doing around here?" Abi said she was there to get a green card and in five years she would be able to apply. Linda asked how she could stand it until then, and Abi tactfully answered, "Well, it's the new South."

There are days when she wants to pack up and leave, especially when a patient looks suspiciously at her in the ER or when someone mispronounces her last name. Dr. Cox, the ER director, calls her Dr. Abi. "I don't do well with foreign names," he said. "You'll have to," she said, "if Obama makes it to the White House."

Cox looked bemused. He isn't quite old enough to be her father and is already beginning to walk with a waddle. He drinks his coffee out of an Ole Miss mug. She has figured out how she gets away with being rude to him. Canada is the only country he has traveled to overseas, so he thinks she sounds British, and, to him, the British are quirky. He is not bad to work with, but Fernandez refers to him as Dr. KKK.

She falls asleep to the smell of curry. The next morning, there is a knock on her door, and she rolls over to check the digital clock. It is 11:27 AM.

Housekeeping

"Housekeeping," someone calls out.

"I'm not ready," she mumbles.

The person knocks again, so she gets up and goes to the peephole. The cleaner is a Latina.

"Housekeeping end at twelve," she says.

"Give me thirty minutes, please," Abi says.

She hobbles back to bed, but she can't fall asleep, so she sits up and calls the front desk.

"Front desk."

"Yes, this is room 218. Is it true housekeeping services end at twelve?"

"No. You can have housekeeping services anytime, ma'am."

"Are you sure? Someone just knocked on my door and she said housekeeping ends at twelve."

"No, ma'am, you can have housekeeping anytime you want."

"Thanks."

The receptionist isn't the same man from last night. She guesses this one is white American, but she can't be sure. The curry smell is stale now. She decides she will move to another suite today, but first she will take a shower. She needs to go to a Nigerian grocery store nearby to buy provisions like yams and palm oil. She can get her habaneros and platanos from the Wal-Mart in Pine Springs. She also has to go to the Lennox Square Mall to buy a white shirt for B.J.'s party.

After her shower, she changes into jeans and a T-shirt and calls the front desk again. It is now 12:44 PM.

"Yes, this is room 218. I was the one who called about housekeeping a while ago. Can you please send someone over now?"

"Yes, ma'am," the receptionist says.

"Thanks."

She turns on the television to the "Entertainment Starts Here" menu and channel-hops from ABC, to FOX, to CNN. It is just the usual posturing about the presidential primaries. Obama is in the lead. She switches the television off when she hears a knock on the door. It is the Latina cleaner.

"Hello," Abi says.

The cleaner doesn't respond or smile. She wears brown scrubs with the hotel logo, and her hair is in a bun secured with a ballpoint pen. She leaves her cart by the door and walks in carrying a blue plastic caddy. She takes a short brush from the caddy and goes into the bathroom to clean the toilet. A couple of minutes later, she flushes the toilet and begins to scrub the sink with the same brush.

Abi imagines the feces, urine and blood the brush harbors.

"Excuse me," she asks. "Didn't you just use that brush for the toilet?"

The cleaner shakes stray hairs from her forehead. Abi hears footsteps in the corridor. An Indian man walks by, white shirt tucked in and hands in pockets. He glances at her as he passes her door and hastily looks away. Does she appear angry? She raises her hand to signal to the cleaner to stop and calls the front desk yet again.

"Hello, this is room 218. You sent a cleaner over and I'm not pleased with the way she's cleaning my room."

"Why?"

A sigh has crept into his voice, as if she is becoming troublesome, as if he now fully realizes she is not from around here.

Abi raises her voice. "She used her toilet brush for my sink. I'm sorry, but I'm a doctor and that is an E. coli epidemic waiting to happen. People can die from E. coli. I would like to speak to your manager about this, please."

The receptionist sounds as if he is standing up. "The housekeeping manager?"

"That will do."

"One moment, ma'am. I will connect you."

She sits on the bed and crosses her legs. The cleaner returns to the cart in the corridor and waits there. The manager picks up after several beeps.

"Housekeeping?"

"Yes, I'm calling from room 218. Listen, I'm not looking for any trouble here, but I've just seen your cleaner use the same brush for the toilet and sink. I think that is terribly, terribly dangerous."

"You say what now?"

"Your cleaner. She used the same brush for my toilet and sink."

"She did what now?"

"She used the same brush for my toilet and sink. I don't want trouble, but I'm a doctor and I'm, uh, very concerned about this."

"Concerned" shows she is serious but not angry.

"I am so sorry. They are not supposed to do that."

"I know."

"We train them."

"I'm sure."

"Some of them don't speak English."

"It's not about that."

"I'll take care of it. Is she still there?"

"She's in the corridor."

"Okay, I will beep her. What room did you say you was in?"
"218."
"Wait."

The manager is definitely an African American woman. In the corridor, the cleaner leans on her cart. Abi imagines her retaliating by using her toothbrush to scrub the toilet. Femi was right; she is germophobic. She can't leave her suite until this is over. The cleaner's beeper goes off and she hears the manager's voice again.

"Ma'am?"
"Yes?"
"She's coming over. I just beeped her. What is your name so I can file a report?"
"Dr. Ogedengbe."
"Huh?"
"I'll spell it."

She has never learned the phonetic alphabet. O for Ostrich, she says, G for Graduate, E for Eagle. She can't think of an N word except for Nigerian.

She finishes spelling her name and notices that the cleaner has abandoned the cart in the corridor, so she goes to her door and shuts it. Afterward, she sits on the sofa, but she misjudges how low and hard it is. As she rubs her thigh, someone knocks on the door. This time she opens the door without looking through the peephole and it is the cleaner, who wipes away her tears with the back of her hand.

"What happened?" Abi asks.
"No more job," the cleaner says as she walks in.
"Why?"

The cleaner shrugs. Abi checks the corridor and there is

no one in sight. She hurries back to her bedside and calls the front desk. There is no reply. She slams the phone down and sits on her bed.

"Crud," she says. She picked up this slang from Cox.

The cleaner carries her caddy to the sink. She pours a liquid from the plastic container and the smell of bleach spreads around the suite. A wall obscures what she is doing. Abi leans over to get a full view and she spots her toothbrush safely in its case when the phone rings, startling her. It is the manager.

"Um, Doctor?"

"I've been trying to reach you," Abi says.

"Is she there yet?"

"Yes, but I think she is saying she is going to lose her job. Why?"

"She knows not to do that."

"Yes, but please don't fire her over this."

"She knows not to do that."

"It's not necessary."

"We trained her."

"Maybe she just didn't understand you."

"Huh?"

"Maybe she misunderstood you?"

"Well, we trained her."

"Okay, okay."

Abi hangs up. All she has in her bag is a twenty-dollar bill. She toys with the idea of giving it to the cleaner as a tip. Will the cleaner accept it? She reaches for her bag on the table on the empty side of the bed.

The cleaner finishes and Abi hands over the twenty-dollar bill and murmurs, "Gracias."

The cleaner takes it and returns to her cart without saying a word. Abi shuts the door and goes back to bed. She is tired. She has been tired since she moved to America. She could easily fall asleep in the position she is in, but for the overwhelming smell of bleach.

ACKNOWLEDGEMENTS

Many thanks to my publisher, Michel Moushabeck; to David Klein, Pam Fontes-May and the team at Interlink; and to my copy-editor, Sue Tyley.

ABOUT THE AUTHOR

Sefi Atta is the author of the novels *Everything Good Will Come*, *Swallow*, *A Bit of Difference*, *The Bead Collector*, *The Bad Immigrant*, *Good-for-Nothing Girl*; a collection of short stories, *News from Home*; and *Sefi Atta: Selected Plays*. She has received several literary awards, including the 2006 Wole Soyinka Prize for Literature in Africa and the 2009 Noma Award for Publishing in Africa.